THE STORY OF EARTH

ACCORDING TO SPRKLE, A YOUNG SPIRIT

PATRICIA L. RITCHIE

Copyright © 2023 by Patricia Ritchie. All rights reserved.

All rights reserved. No part of this book may be reproduced or transmitted in any form or by any means, electronic or mechanical, including photocopying, recording, or by any information storage and retrieval system without express written permission from the author, except in the case of brief quotations embodied in critical reviews and certain other noncommercial uses permitted by copyright law.

Published in the United States of America

Brilliant Books Literary
137 Forest Park Lane Thomasville
North Carolina 27360 USA

CONTENTS

INTRODUCTION

We did not come from apes or monkeys.

Human are human, and apes are apes—two separate species entirely.

I sincerely hope that one day one enlightened scientist would wake up and start to dig deep enough to find out about the truth.

So far, information being taught in the world at large about apes as humans is all theory; and one thing is sure, and even the scientists admit, that the genetic imprints of human and apes are not 100 percent compatible. This means there is a difference, and this is the all-important key to new thinking.

I look up at the stars and the open sky from horizon to horizon, and I see that Earth is floating through space, totally open to life on the solar, and even galactic systems. Earth is not alone, and Earth is a living entity. I cannot imagine that Earth as a living being and not communicating and exchanging and trading with other star systems in a way that our scientist are not yet able to discover. I cannot imagine that Earth had not had visitors from other star systems during its billions of years of existence.

Somehow, the Red Indians, the ancient Egyptians, even ancient Tibetan cultures knew about the star quality of the human species and also the stellar interconnectedness of the solar, the galactic, and the universe and cosmos.

In view of this, I believe deeply that human's origin came from the stars and animals, like apes and other same species, were introduced and evolved more on ground level. I also believe that each species has an important role to play on this planet and we are all interdependent for our very survival within the Wheel of Life here.

In this book I would like to offer a different viewpoint, an alternative theory if you like, about the origin of human race and even a bit further than that, the origin of planet Earth and our solar system.

Children can read this as a magical story, and adults can read this and form their own opinion, because there are many layers in this text that you can play with.

I am writing with book in partnership with my Higher Selves and Guides in spirit just like my other previous books. So this is a joint venture project from all of us, hoping to bring forth some inspiration and deeper thoughts into the truth about our existence.

Many people are asking today:

"Who am I really, and why am I here?"

"What is my purpose?"

An ancient sage said, "Search and you will find. Knock and doors will open for you."

CHAPTER 1

THE SPIRIT WORLD

O nce upon a time, deep in the heart of the central sun of the grand heaven, there was a big *bang*. The sound was so loud that it could be heard throughout the whole universe and beyond. Suddenly, from the centre of the blinding brilliance millions of little balls of light like fireworks spewed out in all directions, filling the sky with a kaleidoscope of colours.

These little balls of light are called spirits. They come directly from the Source of all Life in the universe. They carry within them the Love/ Light/Life energy of the One Creation that allows everything to exist and develop infinitum. Because of this energy, spirits that are born from this centre never die. They live for eternity.

Among the many newborn spirits, there was one very special to us. His name was Sprkle. He looked like a transparent ball with pure white light in the middle.

He (*for the sake of easy reading I just choose a gender, a male gender. But one must understand that light is just light*) was young and full of energy, and his movements were swift and sudden. His fire and light would flare here and there wildly. Sometimes he shrank his body to the size of a pinhead, and other times he expanded to a huge ball. Sometimes, like a laser gun, he would shoot his light in all directions at the same time. He just could not control himself.

Soon a bigger sphere arrived. The colour of this light was a bit different from Sprkle's. It was white and lemon yellow, lined with a touch of blue on the top. This sphere of light had a strong female element in her energy. Her name was Nan. Her movement was slower, very controlled, and elegant. Her nature was loving, very kind and gentle. She loved to take care of the young ones, and so she was assigned to look after the newborn spirits.

After the big-bang birth, she would go around collecting the little ones and bring them to a special sphere called the Cradle. There they would be nourished with tender loving care and given lessons on how to control and work with their energy.

Inside Cradle they would live for some time, to learn all things regarding the understanding of vibrations, forms and structures, and how to control their own energy and light within themselves. They would also learn how to live with each other as a group. There would be teachers and guides who would fly in from other worlds to share knowledge and help each young spirit to develop to its full potential.

In this world, all communication was done telepathically. Information would be transferred from mind to mind directly.

Even though newborn spirits were all white in colour, they could recognise each other through their individual light frequencies, which is different from everyone else. When an individual spirit matures with more acquired knowledge and experiences, the colour and frequencies would change. The new colour continues to change according to the stages of growth of the Spirit.

Teachings and learnings were conducted with the highest respect given to individual freedom of thoughts and choices.

There were halls of music, of colours, of art, and many wonderful things. In the Hall of Experiment, Sprkle and his mates would learn about control of energy matter, dark matter and light matter, creating forms with matter, changing forms by changing the frequencies of the sound and the light, and how to use symbols, and so forth.

There was no time restriction or dateline to meet. All learning progress was implemented according to individual needs, and much time was given for group fun and games.

On many occasions there would be lessons on travel and exploration. This was Sprkle's favourite subject. Students who had chosen this subject would be brought to a hall with rows of seats. Right in front was a huge panoramic screen, 360 degrees surrounding the space. Images on the screen were alive, and everything moved according to the actual event on a given program. This hall was called the Galactic Scanner.

So before going off to any specific star system. The teacher would prepare a program where students could zoom into that particular system and study all the structures and other interesting aspects of the planets and stars. Afterwards, they would make the actual visit.

They would learn how to fly long distance by reducing their bodies into tiny specs of lights and travel everywhere using the light waves from different suns. They would study the locations of different star gates in the universe and travel through them. They could jump from one galaxy to another or one star system to another. On some occasions they would learn to use the Mind Travel Method so that they could reach their destination instantly through thoughts.

In the wonderful world of Cradle, everyone and everything lived in perfect harmony, utmost respect, and deep love for all.

"All is One and One is All" was the unspoken motto in this world.

Everywhere he went Sprkle could feel a mysterious Presence that one could not see, but everyone and everything could feel it very deeply within the very core of their being. In this Presence, one could feel love, light, peace, joy, harmony, and a sense of oneness with everything and everyone. This Presence seemed to be the core magnet that held everything in the universe together. It just felt like home.

Purple Flame

In the Halls of Learning every young spirit would be assigned a spiritual teacher. Once a teacher accepts a student, and the student accepts the teacher. This relationship will be maintained for a long time. The teacher would try his/her best to teach, help, support, guide—in short, do everything he/she could to make sure that the student would live and evolve to his/her fullest potential.

One day Sprkle saw Nan floating toward him from a distance. She was coming to visit him. She was accompanied by something or someone he could not see clearly. He saw a flowing field of light. The colour was deep blue and lilac. At first this had no form. As they approached this blue light, it became an old man. He had long white hair and beard. He wore a long purple robe lined with golden threads.

Telepathically Nan informed Sprkle that he had a new teacher and his name was Purple Flame.

Purple Flame was a very wise and knowledgeable spirit, because he had spent millions of years travelling to many different worlds and many galaxies as a galactic explorer.

In order to experience the life of a local planetary creature, he had taken different forms including animals, birds, rocks, even chemical gases and other indescribable species.

Sprkle was delighted to have a teacher with such wide knowledge. He looked forward to learn much from him because he had a very curious mind. He constantly had more than ten questions dancing about in his mind, and he was always looking for answers. He wanted to know about everything.

One day Sprkle asked, "Teacher, since you are a galactic explorer, could you tell me more about your experiences? I am curious and would like to learn more about life in other worlds. From the Galactic Scanner I have seen worlds very different from ours, especially the third dimensional worlds, where gravitational force is strong and everything is slow and heavy and the matters there are more solid.

"Also, I have learnt that there is a solar system called Sol and one of its planet is Earth, where there are diseases and killings and people cannot fly without machines. That seems to be a very terrible and challenging place to be. I would like to know more about that place. Have you been to Earth before?"

"My dear," Purple Flame spoke, "I am very happy that you have this desire to learn more. According to your development progress, it is indeed time for you to step out of the Home system and face some real challenges. Without these challenges, you can never change and evolve into higher wisdom. The best way to acquire knowledge is through experience.

"Within the galaxy called the Milky Way, there are billions of stars and planets, each with its own characteristic and offer great opportunities for learning. Indeed, the Sol system and its planets have a long and violent history. This whole corner of the Milky Way has been chosen for great experiments involving both the power of darkness and the power of the light.

"The creatures of the Dark Force have been allowed to rule and run to its destructive limit, and many low vibrational beings from this side have been invading and colonising many other star systems in this area. The strong exploiting the weak and so many evil deeds have been committed. Not only Sol, but the whole lower left quadrant of the Milky Way galaxy is covered with a very strong shield of dark energy.

"Occasionally the Elders of the Celestial Realms would send Warriors of Light to repair and heal when too much destruction had been done to some areas, trying to bring balance. Unfortunately, much work is still needed and success is still quite far off the mark. So, for this reason, going to Earth will definitely speed up your learning time because of the challenges involved. But I warn you, it is a very difficult and dangerous undertaking. Many of our students in the past could not endure the physical hardship and sufferings they experienced there and opted to cut short their agreed timeline time by committing suicide or were lost in the dark world for eons.

"You must research deeper and ponder on this idea carefully before you make your decision. Remember, this is only your first journey outside your home sphere and you are not at your full strength yet."

Having heard those words of wisdom, Sprkle said, "Well, I think it is better to be prepared before I make any decision. Meanwhile, can you answer some questions?"

When was Earth created and why?
Who was the first human race and why were they created?
What is the cause of this evil and violence?
When and how did it all started?

These and many other questions were dancing in his mind; and finally, he said, "I need to know everything from the beginning. Teacher, please help me."

Having heard Sprkle's questions and request, Purple Flame went to ask the permission from the Elders in the Celestial Realm to allow Sprkle to enter the Hall of Universal Remembrance, where he will get all the answers that he was looking for.

Permission was given, then Purple Flame drew a symbol in the ether with his mind. This symbol was the key to open the portal to another dimension, and with a small movement, Sprkle had arrived at the entrance of the Hall of Records.

He was surprised to see that the Hall of Universal Remembrance was actually not a big room but rather it was an enormous holographic multilayered and multidimensional world. There were worlds within worlds within worlds, layer by layer, going on and on without end.

Everything in this world was living and pulsating with life—pictures, symbols, mathematic equations, geomancy, images of all kinds of landscape of different worlds, creatures, and plants. Sprkle could see images of thoughts, the images of intentions, and colours of emotions. There were energy fields of every planet, every star, every galaxy, every universe, and so forth and so on—all connected through multiple energy lines like a massive net of light called the Matrix.

This was the records of everything that had passed, everything that is still evolving and infinite potentials for the future in all the universes. This was not a hall but an enormous world of memories and probabilities.

There was no beginning and no end here.

Having seen this, Sprkle was overwhelmed and did not know how or where to begin his search. Just when he was feeling confused, Purple Flame directed him to a small section in a lower corner of the huge sphere. Then he made some movement with his hand, and he was able to retrieve a holographic disk that contained the story of Tara and humanity and related subjects. He then gave it to Sprkle to study.

Purple Flame cautioned, "My dear Sprkle, in the universe there are many parallel worlds and time lines with infinite probabilities and possibilities. What you will be seeing now is just one that you have chosen to follow. Your friend may pick up a parallel time line and may discover a totally different story. It is up to you to decide what is the truth for you. Do you understand?"

Sprkle answered, "Yes, Teacher, I will keep this in mind. Thank you."

The teacher passed his hand on the disk, issued a commanding word, and the holographic pictures sprang to life. Instead of watching a movie in the ether, Sprkle found himself as one of the holographic moving images. He was in.

And so a new adventure began.

Tara

Sprkle found himself as a small orb of light hovering in space somewhere in the fifth dimension, observing a nearby planet. From a distance it looked like a bright-green-and-blue marble. It looked interesting because this reminded him of planet Earth in the galactic scanner. He zoomed in and found that this was another planet in different time and space. Earth was in the third dimension, and this planet was in the fifth. This was Tara.

Sprkle marvelled at the huge spectre of lights covering everywhere on this planet and the soft music in the atmosphere. The mountains were multicoloured crystals, the valleys covered with beautiful lush gardens and rolling green hills. There were huge forests where trees were as tall as the sky, even piercing through the clouds. Their leaves were green, orange, red, blue, and even purple colour. They were of many shapes and sizes.

The magical elves and fairies built their homes deep into the forests. There were tiny little colourful mushroom homes for the gnomes. The ferries lived in flower houses. The elves were bigger creatures; therefore, they lived in grand palaces among the trees and leaves. They lived high up near the treetops among the clouds. There were inviting stairs and paths made of flowery vines and twisted roots leading to different cottages that were hung from the tree branches high up. Fireflies and amber lights spread everywhere, like sparkling stars.

There were gnomes, fairies flapping their little wings, flying about, attending and caring for the soil, the plants, and everything that were living in this world.

This was the Plant Kingdom.

Next, Sprkle saw many land creatures. They lived mainly on open fields. They appeared in all kinds of features and sizes, some with many legs and some none. Some with many heads and some with nine pairs of eyes. Others were blind, and some were the tiniest of insects. The big ones were as big as a small hill. Some animals had orange-and-red hair all over the body, and some had blue-coloured hair. These creatures had no legs. Some had no hair at all, and their skin was like a colourful painting of intricate design. Most of the creatures were etheric in nature. They did not have solid bodies. They all sort of floated about a few inches above the ground.

Then there was the Water Kingdom—the vast oceans and seas. The water was transparent, crystal clear. Here is the home for the big sea creatures.

There were underwater crystal mountains, valleys with colourful rock like plants, even trees. Sprkle saw giant fish with many layers of sharp teeth. Some were black and white, some were deep blue, and others were gold and silver mix and so forth. Some of the sea animals were not fish. They were warm-blooded mammals that happened to live underwater. They were huge, and their colour was gold.

In this water world all creatures communicated with sound. They floated, or they jet speeded everywhere on the surface. All the inhabitants of this wonderful world were floating travellers. They followed warm water currents to practically all parts of the planet. They never stay in one place for long. When the planetary water move, they moved and that was constant.

Here Sprkle also saw transparent angelic beings floating and swimming with all the creatures and tending to the natural environment here. They were the Angelic Guardians of the Water Kingdom.

Then there was the Air Kingdom. The ruler was the Elemental Angels who control the wind, clouds, thunder, and lightning. The big and small birds of the air kingdom live and work closely with the land kingdom. Some land animals could take to air and fly, and some air animals needed to rest on land during their long-flight migration.

Sprkle was mesmerized by the elegance of flapping wings. Some were huge, and some were tiny as bees, gliding freely in the air, the easy flow of the bodies as the wind carried them along an unseen path across the whole planet in every direction.

From their bird's eye view they could see everything and everywhere.

The variety of creatures of the flying population can only be described as immense.

Then there was the Fire Kingdom. This world was deep underground, under the water world. There were small fairies and other vapour-like beings. They were mainly red, yellow, and orange colour. These creatures were living flames. They were colourful gas. Sometimes they appear in groups and created tremendous heat, and even explosions, and sometimes they were a single unit.

These creatures were light in a dark world.

The purpose for their existence was to provide heat and energy for the whole planet and also to monitor the temperature so that it did not go extreme at any time. They rarely come up to the surface, but when they do come up, they would appear as volcanic eruption.

After this overview, Sprkle also wanted to learn about the energetic structure of Tara. He saw that the whole planet was supported by a huge crystal in the shape of a six-pointed star with the outline of a hexagon in the central core, and this provided all the energy that it needed and also served as an anchor of balance, allowing the gentle spin around the planetary axis in certain beat and rhythm in perfect harmony with the universe.

Then from the core crystal, the energy will run through a widespread channel system that covered the whole planet on the surface, and below, every level was being reached. This was the Planetary Energy Grid.

This takes the life force from the core crystal to support and nourish everything on Tara.

The energy from the grid would rise from the core to the surface and many miles beyond into the sky, forming a layer of protective field around the globe. This is called the Planetary Energy Field. This serves like a shield against excessive radiation spewed from other star systems. With this protective shield, the atmosphere could be maintained at a comfortable level at all times.

He also noticed that at different points where the Energy Lei Lines meet, there were interdimensional portals and star gates through which travellers could go to any stars and even galaxies.

In this wonderful world everything seemed to be covered with a thin layer of gold dust. Everything here, whether they be trees or animals, they were all etheric in biological structure. There was telepathic communication among all the creatures in and beyond their respective kingdoms. Trees would be talking to the sea creatures and they in turn could talk to the air creatures and even the crystal mountains would occasionally join in the conversations.

Sprkle wanted some more explanations about Tara, and Purple Flame explained, "Among all the grand stars and zillions of planets in the cosmos, Tara is a new experiment. Experiments and new creations are the pastime of Celestial Beings.

"These Celestial Beings are the titanic collective of cosmic Mind and Power that live mostly in the very high dimensions. They like to spend their time creating universes, nebulas, galaxies, black holes, white holes, stars, star gates, planets, and so forth and all types of creatures within them. Their favourite objective is one word—*variety*. They love varieties. They love changes and movements. That is why you can see that everything in the universe is moving and changing all the time.

"Once they create a universe, they would send the Galactic Guardians and various angels to monitor and manage them so that all their creations would progress and evolve in perfect rhythm and balance."

At this point Sprkle wondered why he was shown this particular planet and how this was connected with the planet Earth, which he was initially interested in and which was supposed to be in the third dimension.

Purple Flame coaxed him, "Look further and you will understand. You have said that you wanted to know everything from the beginning and so here it is. This is going to be an interesting lesson for you."

After those words, *poof*, and he disappeared into thin air.

Meanwhile, Sprkle continued his observation and moved the time in the record forward a couple of million years to one important day.

The First Human Race: The Astral Human

On this day Sprkle observed a group of Elders from the Celestial Realm came hovering on this planet, and they said to each other, "This Tara is evolving very well. It has been a successful experiment so far. It is time to create a higher intelligent species to be the guardian of all the kingdoms here and also to help their evolution further on."

There was unanimous agreement.

After some pondering and discussions, it was decided that this new race would be called Human. They would be the guardian not only of the whole planet and all the creatures living there, they would also be responsible for all the star gates installed there.

Soon the process of creating this new Human race began. It was to be 144,000. That would be the first experimental batch.

Next, the Wise Elders paid a visit to Nan at the Cradle. Nan welcomed the arrival of the Celestial Elders, listened to their request and their plan.

She was to select among the young ones those who were ready to leave the "nest" that had been trained with all the necessary basic lessons and also who were mature enough to handle self-control and responsibilities.

Soon Nan came back with a huge transparent sphere. There were many balls of light sparkling like little stars. They were all uniformly white light. Nan passed this sphere to the Elders, saying, "These ones are ready and suitable for your plan. They are in a state of slumber right now for easy travelling—144,000 of them, the number requested. Take them with my love and best wishes."

The Elders took the sphere with tenderness, thanked Nan, and departed.

Next, the sphere was transported to a special place with a huge crystal dome. This was the place of new creation and experiments. This was the New Life Centre.

The angels in charge here were called Team New Life. They worked in groups. They were experts in life force energy, genetic engineering, symbols, vibrations, frequencies, and different kinds of matters.

Here in this special world anything and everything in the universe can be created and formulated. The only thing they could never create was the Original Life Force of Divine Light.

As soon as the sphere arrived, it was put in an enormous pool full of a special kind of plasma liquid. The little spirits were still in slumber mode, and they were released gently into the warm liquid. They will only be awakened when the whole process was finished.

Without wasting any time, Team New Life started the process of creating a new specie called the human race.

First step: To choose one spirit unit for experiment and test. If all goes well, then they will use this formula to work on the rest.

Second step: To create an over-soul body structure to protect the spirit body. The light of the little spirit, even though small, is still very powerful because they came from the Light of all Lights, the Source of all Creation. The power of this spirit would instantly explode any new body structure if it is not well done.

This is the most delicate part of the whole operation.

To create this over-soul body, they used a layer of pure minute crystalline matter, very refined, to cover the entire spirit light. This is also called the Crystal Body. This serves as a protective shield of the spirit in case of any contamination that may come from external influence. No matter what happens in the future, the spirit and the crystal body will always remain pure and intact. Then they inserted life consciousness into this over-soul body.

Third step: to create another body layer in order to be able to adapt, to live, and function in the fifth dimensional world. This would be the Astral Body. For this they would use a combination of carbon and silica matter for the biological body. They layered this on top of the crystal body. Then this body was also given life consciousness. This crystal body also makes the astral body androgynous. It carries both the male electric energy and female magnetic energy; therefore, it has the best ability to receive and transmit life force current.

Fourth step: to create a thin layer of crystal light covering the astral body. This is called the Personal Energy Field.

This field emits a rainbow light around the body that is called the Auric Light Field. This Auric Light Field have two purposes: one was to provide an extra layer of protection around the astral body and the other purpose was to connect the Personal Energy Field with the Planetary Energy Field of Tara.

The Personal Energy Field of all the creatures are connected with the Planetary Energy Field of a planet, and this field is in turn connected with the Galactic Energy Field which is also connected with the Universal Energy Field. This is how everything is connected as one and everything is connected through the Living Consciousness. This is the Law of One.

The fifth step: was to create a life program, plus all the information that this body needs to function in this life time and put it in a minute chip installed inside the astral body.

Sixth step: since it was intended for this special race to govern all the kingdoms of Tara, as well as the star gates; therefore, it was necessary to provide them with additional program.

The basic power of Love and Light already came with the spirit, so they added the following:

- memories of their divine nature, that they are the children of the One First Creation

- the power to co-create with the most advance technologies available in their respective worlds
- the meaning of the Law of One
- the Maps and Codes to unlock and operate all the star gates for interstellar travel.

The test run was successful, and so the formula was applied to the rest of the sleeping spirits.

And so the spirit light plus the crystal body (the over-soul), plus the astral body (the soul), plus the Personal Energy Field together became Astral Human.

At this point in time Sprkle asked if he could also be one of the Astral Human so that he could experience life on Tara.

Purple Flame obtained permission for this request, knowing that this sojourn will help him grow. With this permission came also a special privilege—the ability to move his consciousness in a body or out of it and go back to the Hall of Record as observer. He could do that because he had been given a special Visitor Pass.

Then Sprkle, as an orb of light (the spirit form), entered the pool with the rest of the orbs and also got the program chip transplanted into his new body.

When everything was done, the final step was to awaken everyone in the pool and soon the New Life Team saw the rising of one rainbow light form with long elegant transparent body and a bright star within.

One by one these beautiful starlight bodies rose from the pool slowly and gently floating in midair until all 144,000 of them plus Sprkle were gathered in the ceiling of the crystal dome like hundreds of thousands of multicolour hanging lamps illuminating the whole hall.

The pure-white diamond cut crystal dome reflected this light out to the sky and beyond, far, far away into the dark space, covering everywhere with sparkling and shimmering rainbows.

This awesome spectrum of light was the announcement of the birth of the first human race. They were the Astral Human Race.

All the angels in heaven and the Wise Elders rejoiced and sang songs in celebration.

After the big party was over, Astral Human group was being transported to Tara and dispersed to various kingdoms on the planet to start a new life cycle.

Astral Human had long elegant transparent bodies, about twenty feet in length. They were both male and female energy. They did not have face because all their communication was done telepathically. They did not need facial expression because everyone else could see through their thoughts and desires. They either floated a few feet above the ground or fly like the wind high up in the sky and were able to shift shape to whatever form they wished.

All the dwellers of the different kingdoms saw the arrival of this wonderful newcomers descending gently from the sky like thousands of warm candlelights. They welcomed them with open arms and songs.

Sprkle as Astral Human travelled far and wide on the planet. When he first came to Tara, he could only observe from the outside, now he was able to actually experience life as one of the inhabitant.

Since he was able to shift shape his body, therefore he tried living as different species in different kingdoms. He had been a bird, a four-legged animal, and even lived as a gaseous flame in the underworld.

Throughout these various lives, he had acquired precious knowledge. He understood that without having lived as a bird, for example, he would never be able to really know what it felt like to *be* a bird or even live inside an egg.

Having acquired the experiences he wanted, Sprkle started to search for the next new thing. Soon he discovered an organization called the Co-Creation Team.

Their short name was CC Team. They introduced new creatures in every kingdom, they managed repair of the affected areas after destructive storms and other unpleasant natural occurrences, they healed animals and plants when they were not well, and they settled disputes among the dwellers of the different kingdoms to ensure the highest level of harmony all around. They also enhanced the beauty among the various kingdoms so that evolution could be brought to a new height.

Sprkle was inspired by the dedication and efficient management of the members of this team, so he joined them. Through the works of this new group, he had learned and done many wonderful things. One day Sprkle decided to return to the holographic base to make further observation.

He saw that with the empathetic guardianship of the Astral Humans, Tara strived for millions of years until she became a beautiful shining jewel and her rainbow auric light around her planetary field shone far and wide.

The Kan Race

In time Tara caught the attention of star travellers from other stellar systems far and near.

Then change came, slowly at first, the planetary Spirit Mother saw more and more spaceships and visitors came from other stars. They were of different races. Even though they were all etheric in their biological structure, they had different forms, shapes, and sizes. None of them looked like Astral Human.

Some came for short visits to explore, and others came to stay. Those who were able to adapt to the local atmosphere stayed longer and lived in harmony with their neighbours. Some small communities came as refugees from dying planets. These came in peace.

Then came an unusually old and powerful race. These were also etheric humanoid, but they had dark auric light field. Unlike the new and young Astral Human, this race was much older, millions of years older, and they had many kinds of mix genetic imprint in their bodies. This race was called Kan.

At this point Sprkle called up his teacher to learn more about the Kan. Purple Flame explained, "They were children of the Fallen Angels called Annu-Elohim who have chosen to be the negative force, opposing the Light. Therefore, they are known as the Dark Force. They had separated themselves from the Christ Consciousness at the eleventh dimension.

Nevertheless, they retained the power of the tenth dimension.

"The Kan race is very experienced and knowledgeable about manipulating energy matters. They are ambitious and cunning. They do not have emotion, and they cannot feel love, which is the essence of God, the Source of Life. They only know about getting power for themselves and dominate others whom they deem weak.

"They had detected the divine light and power of Tara and studied her thoroughly at a distance for a long time. Now they come with the intention of colonizing her. They particularly choose this time to come because they are very interested in the new Astral Human Race. They want to destroy it. "They could see that Astral Human was an angelic race endowed with power and destined to be the guardian of many interstellar star gates. They saw them as a threat, and that is why needed to be taken down.

"Before the Kan landed here, they had already colonized 350 other planets and had control over many star gates in the lower quadrant of this galaxy. After conquering and colonizing a star or planet, they would get everything they want from that place and transport them back to their home base, a star system called the Shadow. This is the headquarters of the Kan empire that stretched far and wide in the local galaxy. They had millions of slaves and also robotics working in mines for all kinds of minerals and materials that they need to run their vast empire. And now they want Tara, the new jewel.

"I suggest you continue to follow this time line and learn more from this point onward. I will leave you now."

On the holographic, Sprkle saw that as soon as the Kan starships landed on Tara, they started to apply their plan to infiltrate the Personal Energy Fields of the peaceful Astral Human population.

The Kan human wanted to harness the high starlight energy of the Astral Human, who were young and full of vitality. They were also easily tricked and manipulated. The lure of power and vast ownership of other stars and planets was very hard to resist, and many naive young Astral Human were no match for the trickeries of the old cunning "foxes," and many fell into the dark trap.

Thousands of time cycles passed, and Sprkel observed that Tara had become a big multiracial melting pot. Apart from the Kan, other beings came from many other star systems. The population was increasing exponentially.

Through merging and mixing of the Personal Energy Fields with different types of creatures the original Personal Energy Fields of the Astral Human changed, not to the better but to the worse.

Their original rainbow light auric fields, which was big and bright before, now they became dimmer, and in some cases even quite dark. The more they mix with the other creatures, especially with the Kan humanoid, the dimmer their light and even their twenty-feet long bodies were getting shorter. Some only had bodies of about nine feet long, the height of the Kan. They became Astral/Kan mix human.

Those with the low vibration and dark auric field were becoming more and more in numbers. This group was slowly rising to become the dominant ruler of a vast area of the land by gradually eating up other smaller communities especially the more passive and peaceful ones.

There was a small group in the population that was also protected and managed to maintain their angelic form and the divine light within. This group was assigned the mission as the Guardians of the Maps and Codes of the twelve star gates that were originally installed in various parts of Tara.

The Subraces

Meanwhile, Sprkle moved the time line forward and saw that the population of Tara, despite occasional conflicts, continued to grow and mix until the original races that came earlier had evolved into various subraces.

One of the major subrace was more peaceful and had more magical slant, and they were called On Yan. This group, although they were also mixed, had more original Astral Human energy in them. They were ten feet long, and they had green, yellow, and orange auric light fields around them. The other major subrace was called the Kong Yan. They had more Kan plus other diverse elements in their energy field. As a result of this mixing of genes after millions of years, this race had lost the original human form. They had a black menacing-looking bird head, a human torso, and had hands and feet of claws. They were about nine feet tall. They were ambitious and had aggressive personalities. They devoted more time in free experimentations and development of advance technology for self-serving purposes.

In the beginning, the land and various kingdoms of Tara was shared as one. All planetary dwellers enjoyed total freedom of movement and migration. Now, due to differences in culture and beliefs, they lived apart and built walls and fences.

In order to avoid serious conflict, these two major tribes were separated far from each other and smaller communities occupied different parts of the land.

As the Wheel of Time turned, Sprkle saw that the more spiritual and peaceful On Yan lived in harmony with all their neighbours, be they human or not. They worked to tend to their environment, always promoting growth and new products to improve health and positive living, and so they prospered. Sprkle loves art and music, and he could see beauty and abundance everywhere in this community.

On the other hand, the more aggressive Kong Yan were creating higher technological machines and instruments to harness ever more power. They were becoming more dominant in the community, and their numbers was also increasing very quickly.

There were constant quarrels and conflicts even among their own tribes due to power struggle, jockeying for the leadership position.

Sprkle saw that on the Kong Yan part of the land the once green forests and gardens they were replaced by stone-cold grayish buildings. They were big fortresses and castles with high walls and spiky metal spires stuck out everywhere. There were huge factories for weapons and enormous fire burners everywhere, spewing out chunks of choking black smoke all the time. These factories never stop. Fire, metals, and slaves work nonstop, producing loads and loads of weapons. There was fumes and dark smoke everywhere. It was a sight of hell.

Sprkle moved forward the time cycle to one important day.

He saw that the Kong Yan's technological experiments had reached a point when they could extract power from Tara's main crystal generator in the planet's centre. This was the major power that supported the whole planet.

Sprkle was horrified. Then he also saw a plan laid out to issue an all-out attack on all the subraces and take control of the whole planet. Having learned about this, Sprkle immediately changed back into the Astral Human body and went to alert the Co-Creation Team, who in turn informed the community so that they could make preparation for evacuation. Next, the C Team asked for help from the Galactic Council who sent angels in charge of crisis and security. Soon a mass evacuation of the population was being organized.

Sprkle stayed behind to help with the evacuation. The Guardians of the Maps and Codes also stayed behind. They will do everything they could to safeguard the star gates.

Soon the Dracos and the Reptilian race, came from other systems to expand their networks. And together with the Kong Yan tribe they formed an association of various warlike races. They called themselves the POWR Federation. This federation collectively owned and control vast empires covering very large area of the Milky Way galaxy.

They feel that now they were strong enough even to rebel against the Celestial Elders. They wanted to capture the Astral Human, Guardians of the Maps and Keys, to take control of the star gates for themselves and to expand to other parts of the galaxy.

Here Sprkle needed some explanation as to why there is so much hunger for power and aggression in the Kong Yan and other similar races, and Purple Flame came to enlighten him.

He said, "In order to prevent any interference of their grand plan of invasion and colonization in the galaxies, the Dark Force in the higher dimensions and their creation, the members of the POWR Federation, deliberately cut off permanently their energy field link with the celestial home from the eleventh up to the fifteenth dimension.

"They created an energy shield that cover all over their Personal Energy Field so that the vibration and telepathic communication with the High Celestial Realm was no longer possible. Not only that, they also apply this Dark Energy Field on all the conquered planets and star systems so that no light rays can penetrate them and they will remain in darkness and under their full mind control. Their slaves are just like living zombies.

"The original Astral Human, on the other hand, through their spiritual light, could evolve to the fifteenth dimension and beyond that go back to God. But the members of the POWR Federation could only reach the tenth dimension. This is the highest point of evolution they could achieve. "From this point forward they would be known as the Fallen Angels because they are still of angelic nature or the Dark Force. And those who remain loyal to God, the Light and Love, would be known as the Force of Light."

Here Sprkle needed some more explanation about the meaning of Darkness versus Light, and Purple Flame went on. He said, "It is through the constant replenishing of the Life/Love/Light from God Source to the spirit and soul that all creation can live and develop.

"This is the fundamental element of all God's children so that no matter how far away the souls may wonder in the universe, the spirit will always lead them back home to God. The spirit never dies. The spirit lives forever and ever just like God.

"The Dark Force is not able to access this Life/Light from the Source because of the shield that they imposed on themselves, and so when their life cycle is over, they would die and turn to cosmic dust. In order for them to continue to live they needed to suck this Life/Light from the beings that carry them. That is why the Dark Force is also known as the Vampires. That is why they need to be constantly looking for different life beings to conquer them, to control them, and, more importantly, to eat them. They feed on their Life essence so that they can live longer. What they are doing is actually to secure their own survival."

After these wise words from his loving teacher, Sprkle was once again enlightened. He continued to monitor the ongoing drama of what was to him now his favourite planet, Tara.

Soon war broke out and quickly spread to various parts of the planet. It was between the POWR Federations and the Angelic Warriors. Also involved in the battles were the Guardians of the Maps and Codes and some Astral Human who opted not to leave. He also saw that one of the major star gate was captured by the POWR.

Meanwhile, the evacuation was still going on, and Sprkle was concerned as there were more and more Taran queuing up to depart. Some needed spaceships to travel, and others could just use light waves. But whatever means of travel, still organization and order was needed to maintain safety for everyone. Sprkle was very busy working with the C team.

One day a group of the POWR Federation was trying to force open one of the star gates that they captured. They got the Map, but they did not have the Keys that required specific codes in order to open. They devised an alternative plan to extract enough electrical power from the planetary core crystal to force open the gate. They took too much.

Suddenly, a tremendous explosion with blinding light and thundering sound occurred. Thereafter, a series of minor explosions followed, destroying the greater part of the planetary energy grid.

Vast areas and most of the Kong Yan's constructions were obliterated. A small number of their elite members were able to leave just in time and went back to their homeland, the Shadow, but the majority of their tribe and slaves were blown to dust.

The first big explosion had torn off a big chunk of the planet's crust and hurled it into space. Afterwards Mother Tara saw that her body had a big hole in the centre. And with the core crystal generator damaged, instead of rotating on her axis as usual, it started to wobble for a short while and finally stopped moving all together.

More destructive forces subsequently came in the form of fire, smoke, and water; and these elements were flooding, burning every living thing along their path. Even the air was not out of the equation. There were massive black clouds, and dust filled the sky for months on end, sucking and choking the living energy of all the creatures of the air kingdom.

At the end, Tara was a sorry sight. A big black hole in the middle of her body, she became crippled and muted and she could no longer sustain life. In view of this dilemma, the Galactic Council called up the Angelic Rescue Team to repair the planetary core generator, the energy grid, and other urgent needs.

It would take at least over ten thousand years of major repair works before Tara would be able to move and rotate around her axis again, even so only slowly and weakly. Without the lost land, she remained crippled. Meanwhile, Sprkle was shocked to find his astral body, together with some other Taran, were stuck to a piece of land being hurled into the sky at rocket speed.

They were caught by surprise. The first explosion came so suddenly that they were not able to escape in time, and so they found themselves drifting and tumbling aimlessly. They did not know where they were and where they were heading. One thing they knew for certain, and that was they could not return to Tara anymore. No one could. All they could see was dark space in front. It seemed a very long time had passed, and no rescue was in sight. Sprkle stayed on with the rest of the Taran and waited. The power of the explosion that tore off the land was so great that it was being ejected at laser beam speed into space. The tremendous force and heat broke it into pieces even while speeding. By the time everything slowed down, there were twelve fragments of different sizes and shapes floating into every direction in dark space. Sprkle was sitting on one of them.

In time he saw at a distance the flickering light of the Rescue Team approaching. He knew that his companions will be safe, and he decided to change into a ball of light and return to home base. But something was wrong. Tried as he might he felt limp and lack of energy. He could not change into any other shape or form, he had no power. Telepathically he cried out to Purple Flame for help.

The Teacher came and extended his hand toward the spirit light of Sprkle, and with his own power increased the life force energy of the etheric body of his student, who felt he was fully charged. Together they transformed into two specs of light, and almost immediately they were back in home base.

Soon he was looking at holographic images of the horrible state of devastation that descended upon Tara, and he could not help but cried with deep sadness. This kind of violent destruction on such a big scale shook him to his very core. He had never even imagined that this could happen. He was utterly overwhelmed with emotions.

Seeing Sprkle like this, Purple Flame came to console him. This time Purple Flame adopted the form of a light-green-and-pink blanket of warm light energy and wrapped around his student, so young and innocent.

Sprkle questioned, "What happened to me when I was trapped in the land fragment? Why did I feel so weak?"

Teacher once again explained, "The explosion was so great that Tara's Planetary Life Force Field was damaged, causing rapid leakage of life energy of everything and everyone around her. That is why you could not shift shape as normal. Well, all is not lost. There is a good plan ahead. In order for the full restoration of the damages on the planet, she will need the assistance of a grand salvation plan in which a future tiny planet called Earth will play a part. Just keep following the story."

On hearing the word *Earth*, Sprkle's natural curiosity perked up again. He said, "What could all this chaos have to do with Earth?"

EARTH

The Morning After

Tara, the grand and beautiful planet in the fifth dimension, the birthplace of the first Astral Human Race, experienced many planetary explosions that wiped out most of the living creatures there. One massive explosion tore off a chunk of the planet's land surface and hurled it into space where it fragmented into many pieces.

The Guardians of the highest level in the Celestial Realm were monitoring the cataclysmic event. They could not have done anything to prevent it because it was an accident that occurred suddenly.

All they could do was to call up the Angelic Rescue Team to devise a plan. They knew that the fragments of Tara would not be able to sustain the high frequency that the fifth dimension required and if not rescued soon they would all turn into space dust. If this happens, then the planet would never be made whole again. It is vital that all the missing pieces must be brought back to the planet for full integration and only then that the whole planet could continue to evolve in line with the Law of Ascension.

Meanwhile, the Angelic Team called up thousands of huge spaceships from the nearby star systems for the operation of collecting the variety of beings and creatures that were trapped on the broken land still in space and to bring them to a temporary Healing Zone, which was being prepared to receive them. In time, with proper repair and when the damaged creatures were strong enough to carry the fifth dimensional frequency, then, and only then, could they be brought home. At this point everything and everyone was leaking energy.

Next the Angelic Rescue Team turned their attention to the broken land fragments, which were twelve pieces in various sizes and shapes. They found them drifting in empty space, and they used enormous spaceships to haul them into a special zone. They were all leaking energy and so needed to be brought into a lower dimension with lower vibration.

They soon found an area in a lower part of the Milky Way galaxy, in the third dimension, but before hauling them down the Rescue Angels must ask for the help of the Healing Angels who were in charge of managing vibration and frequencies. They needed to change each and every one of the twelve fragments to the proper frequency before they could be brought into the third dimension; otherwise, they would blow up everything that were in their vicinity. The process needed to be slow and gradual. This operation was so delicate that it took many years to finish.

Here Sprkle asked Purple Flame to explain the following process to help the mending program for Tara.

Purple Flame explained, "It will take many thousands of years for the land fragments to gradually transform into asteroid rocks with the correct vibration to fit the third dimension. However, this was not the end of the process. This was only part of the plan.

"The Guardians knew that it was easier for planets to transform vibrations from high to low, but from low to high they could not do it. The only way was for the individual to do it by its own effort. That means each asteroid rock, no matter what the size, must be given all the proper elements so that it can evolve into living planets.

"From this basic life-form, they must each evolve through their own consciousness and effort. From low to high, they must each climb the steps, one dimension at a time. This will take hundreds of millions or even billions of years, but this is the only way.

"Each rock will be turning around its own axis and then will orbit around a sun, which served as an anchor, and through its magnetic field, it would keep all planets within a stable orbit at a stable beat and rhythm. "And so the next target was to find a suitable sun whose magnetic field was strong enough to hold the balance of the twelve fragments together. They plan to start a solar system in the lower quadrant of the Milky Way, somewhere quiet, far from the other big star clusters. There they found an existing new star that had no planet yet and mature enough to take on the Tara's 'babies' to start a new family.

"The next step, the Angelic Rescue Team merged one piece of the fragments with the sun, matching the frequency there, and subsequently they worked on each of the remaining eleven planets.

"They gave each one specific energy field that enveloped the land, protecting it from over radiation, and at the same time, through the universal matrix, they would be connected with each other and even communicate telepathically so that they would be able to aid each other's evolutionary progress.

"Then according to the natural size and structure of the rocks, the team assigned their individual positions, their orbit time, and rhythm around the sun. Some of the fragments were not stable in their own rotation, and so moons and satellites were brought in to balance their energy. As they were not all the same, therefore some planets would have one moon and some would have several moons and or satellites.

"After everything was done, the planets were allowed to develop in their different ways according to their individual energetic field, environment, and so on. But all of them carried Tara's planetary energy blueprint, and one day will integrate with her again.

"The final integration is crucial because without that Tara's planetary field would not be able to grow strong enough to match the frequencies of the seventh dimension, where she must ascend to meet with her sister planet Gaia according to the Universal Law of Evolution."

Here, Sprkle was curious about progression of souls and planets and about ascension.

The patient teacher further explained, "Well, to learn about the Universal Law you must first know what is a universe. A universe is a creation by the Life-Giving Light, Source. He first created a world of the highest vibrational frequencies followed by music and full spectrum of light. This is the first materialized manifestation of the Life/Light Essence. "Then within this world another world was created. This one carried a lower frequency so that the two worlds would not penetrate each other. This is the first world of the universe. This is the fifteenth dimension, a level closest to the Source. This dimension, plus the fourteenth and the thirteenth, are pure Life-giving Energy. This is group identity of titanic life force.

"Next, within this world another world is created. This is the twelfth dimension, and again its frequency is different so that it remains separate. Following this would be the eleventh, tenth, and so forth until the first dimension, the lowest in frequency.

"The twelfth dimensional universe is called the Time Matrix. This onion-like spheres within spheres, or worlds within worlds, make up one universe. Within this universe, spirits and souls can have single unit identity or group identity if so choose. And you may notice that all these worlds were inside the biggest outer layer, which is the energy field of the Source of all Life. Some may call this the Source, some may call this God, others may know it by the name of the One or All That Is, and so forth.

"Sprkle, are you following me so far?"

"Yes, but what about the law? Did God impose this law? Why?" "You may notice that everything in space turns, spins, and rotates and everything moves with pulse. The pulsation goes in and out, contracting and expanding. Change is constant. Nothing remains the same. Everything runs in cyclical pattern. What goes up must come down, and what is down must go up again to complete a full cycle.

"All life within this universe runs in cycles, and there are small cycles and big cycles. So if a living being was created in the fifteenth dimension, in order to run a cycle, it must go down to experience one life in the fourteenth dimension and then the next life will be in the thirteenth dimension, and so forth. This is called a life cycle.

"This being must go down the ladder of each dimension until the first dimension. Thereafter, it will need to climb the dimensional ladder to the second level, the third, and so forth. And when it reaches the twelfth dimension, it has completed a full cycle called the Spiritual Cycle. Beyond this realm, it will return Home to God, the First Creator.

"There are also many cosmoses and universes and other dimensions beyond the fifteenth and other worlds, but that is another story. For now, a twelve-dimensional universe is sufficient and relevant to what you wish to learn.

"Going down the ladder is called Devolution, and the journey going back up to God is called Evolution or Ascension. This is the Law of the Universe. This is not really a law that God impose on his creatures, but rather an act of love. Like a loving Father/Mother, God let go his children to go forth to experience the worlds, all the worlds in the fifteenth dimensional universe, and then bring them back to the warm embrace of the grandest love of all. As everything is part of God, so everything will naturally return to God. Are you with me, Sprkle?"

"Yes, my great teacher."

"All right now, let us move the time forward to continue the observation and learn."

Having said that, *poof*, and Purple Flame vanished.

Terra

Sprkle moved time forward two hundred million years and observed that the galaxy had a new solar system with one star and eleven planets each orbiting around it in perfect rhythm and harmony. It was beautiful. For the first time after he left Tara, he felt hopeful.

This sun was medium size and just mature in age. It gave out brilliant golden light. This sun was a benevolent and nourishing being. It sent out its life-giving light to all the eleven planets and all their moons covering them like a father embracing his children.

Sprkle marvelled at the beautiful colours of the planets. Each had its own colour pattern with unique personality and consciousness. There was one so big that it was almost the size of the sun itself. He also saw that a small host of guardian angels were assigned to protect, to nourish, and to help the growth of each planet.

These groups of angels were of feminine energy, and they were like mothers. They were Energy of Light, and their colours matched the colours of the planet that they were working on. Some were more red-orange colours, some were green and blue, and so forth.

This kind of angels is called the Compassionate Ones because they are the manifestation of God's Love.

Sometimes these entities appear to humankind in the form of a beautiful lady with bright rainbow halo all around her. She would give them messages of love and kindness and sometimes warning of impending catastrophe. People call this entity Holy Mother, Kuan Yin, Mother of Compassion. They build churches and temples in her honour.

Sprkle also observed that this sun and the planets had names given by the Wise Elders. The sun was named Sol; and the planets were Mercury, Venus, Earth, Mars, Maldak, Jupiter, Saturn, Uranus, Neptune, Pluto, and Nibiru.

After two hundred million years had passed, Tara was sufficiently recovered to sustain life again and it was time for the Angelic Rescue Team to devise a plan to bring home those trapped souls in the Healing Zone. By now some of them were healed and strong enough to return to the fifth dimension. The Angelic Team created a dimensional portal between the Healing Zone and Tara.

A great migration took place where millions of astral beings flew out of the Healing Zone, and by riding the star lights, they sped across space and through the portal to go home. It was a grand sight to behold. Watching this homecoming, Sprkle felt happy and relieved.

After that was done, the Rescue Team turned their attention to Sol and his eleven planets. Even though they had developed into full-fledged planets, there is still the problem of integration.

Sprkle put the issue to his teacher, and he said, "One thing was to rescue souls and astral beings, another was to help the whole solar system. Look on further."

Time passed, and one day the angels had an idea. It was to build a bridge path with a dimensional portal. This bridge would be between the location of the planets in the third dimension and the fifth dimension Tara. This would the best and the fastest shortcut in space, and the portal will have to be on one of the planets nearest to the Bridge.

They would choose one of the eleven planets that was most suitable to install the Bridge. It was decided to be Earth, the third planet from the sun where the temperature and other elements were suitable.

Once decided, Earth was being prepared to serve as a lower version of Tara and bear the name of Terra. All the proper elements were introduced, and over time they were brought to balance and from then on Terra (Earth) was to be the first planet to be seeded with living beings.

Tangia

At this point in time, Terra/Earth was mostly water and one massive piece of land. The name Tangia was given to the land.

First, the sea creatures were introduced and brought in from the nearby planet that was a water world with millions of variety of sea life.

So they brought in whales, dolphins, a few varieties of sharks, stingrays, giant octopus, other medium and smaller fish, cretaceous, and a big variety of underwater plants.

Meanwhile, with a balanced atmosphere small earth plants appeared on the land, the native varieties that were able to sprout as moss and grass and little shrubs. After many years, some trees were able to grow, and gradually, the Guardian introduced other new varieties in order to complete a full natural eco system. After thousands of years, the forest had developed into an enormous plant kingdom, covering the ground and up where the very top of the trees could pierce through the clouds in the blue sky.

Colours were everywhere from the tiniest of bloom to shrub foliage. They were red, blue, yellow, violet, and pink. All these popped up here and there, on top of the general jade-green background.

A view from the clouds, one could see a beautiful multicoloured carpet of living foliage that stretched for miles and miles as far as the horizon, all being nourished by the ever-present golden rays from Sol.

After many years, when the sea creatures were doing well, air creatures were introduced. These were huge flying animals with enormous wings. They could not only fly they could also swim in the sea. There were about a hundred different species of them. When they were not flying or swimming, they would perch on the mountaintop or on the tallest tree branches to rest.

Next, the Angelic Team brought in the gnomes, the fairies, leprechaun, and elves from other star systems to be keepers of the forest, the mountains, and the surrounding sea and its creatures.

Everything on Earth was modelled like the original Tara before the disaster. The only difference was, the atmosphere in third dimension was denser and heavier and everything here was more solid.

The operation went well, and for thousands of years, Terra/Earth was left to develop herself naturally. Meanwhile, the Galactic Guardians were watching and monitoring all aspects on the planet to make sure that everything was in order.

During this time the Galactic Guardians decided that the planet was ready to receive visitors from other star systems, especially the benevolent extraterrestrials who would come with beneficial products and latest technology. The interstellar star gates were installed.

From then on visitors came mostly from the vicinity area. They looked like animals and insectoid, but they were not, they were beings of highly developed intelligence. Some were very old races from very advanced civilizations.

Planet Earth was at this time a new jewel, a young vibrant paradise and attracted much interest from star travellers.

They were curious about this new solar system, and they wanted to explore it.

There were reptiles that walked upright, and they were advance scientists from very old civilization. There were very wise old apes; and there were cats, huge insectoid, bulls, horses, lizards, dragons, and so forth. Some of them were half etheric and half solid. All these being were very big and tall on average. They were about nine to fifteen feet tall.

Each type of these beings had its special expertise on culture, technologies, arts, music, science, and so forth. Some came as refugees from dying planets, some came for adventures, some were transient dwellers, and others were more permanent. These latter ones set up their own buildings and walls. Each group came for different reasons and with their own agendas.

Not all came in peace. Among those who came were the aggressive Kong Yan race who went into exile to the planet Maldack, (between Mars and Jupiter), after the disaster of Tara. They had made this planet their military base.

These warriors were still members of the POWR Federation. They were planning to explore Earth and the local solar system for self-service purposes.

Time passed, and new arrivals mixed with the local natives. And after many generations, the population of Tangia became a big melting pot of a great variety of extraterrestrial creatures and also many different kinds of hybrids. Some of the ETs were fully etheric, and some were half solid and half etheric in body structure.

Those that were more adaptable to water would live in and around the seashore area. Those that prefer higher grounds would live on the mountaintops, and then there were those who liked to live among trees and built their dwellings among the huge branches in the forests.

The Kong Yan and members of the POWR Federation preferred to live away from other communities. They lived mostly in the caves and remote mountain areas.

There were occasional minor conflicts, but since all tribes had their own space and freedom to practice, their way the general condition on the planet was peaceful.

And so for millions of years Earth thrived, and civilization was allowed to flourish.

No human was present at this point in time.

Soul Human

Once again Sprkle moved time forward to the point when the Elders decided to introduce a new race of human to Earth.

After the disaster of Tara, the Elders understood that their creation of Astral Human was flawed in some ways. They did not realize that even though Astral Humans were given high power and knowledge they were not mature. They were young and naive, easily tricked by the cunning older reptilians who knew how to inflate their egos by feeding them with false pride.

This new batch of humanity will be given time to grow and mature so that they will have to acquire strength and wisdom through their own effort and experiences. They will be called Soul Human. Thus a new experiment followed.

Rather than creating a new body structure from scratch like the Astral Human Race, this time Celestial Elders asked the New Life Team (the angelic collective that specialized in genetic engineering to create forms and bodies and hybrids) to create a new version of Astral Human suitable for the third dimensional vibration.

Soul Human, unlike the Astral Human Race whose body was made of light transparent plasma like soap bubble to fit the 5D vibration, this new race was more like water vapour or clouds to fit the third dimension.

This texture was denser and heavier; thus, their vibration much lower than their ancestors.

Since Astral Human already have the God's Spirit Light within their soul structure, the crystal body, the soul body already in place, all that was needed was to lower their 5D frequency to fit 3D frequency. They would be fully etheric and immortal.

After the new sample body was tested and approved, then there would be 14,400 new humans.

Soul Human race would be the descendants of Astral Human Race, meaning they were also connected with Tara. Their bodies would be like an elongated cloud with a head and a pair of eyes.

With the spirit light within, they would be born with full memory of who they were and their connection with their souls and oversouls and the higher dimensions.

Unlike in Tara where all the Astral Human were given the knowledge of the Maps and Keys that had the power to open all the star gates, this time Galactic Guardians decided to separate the Soul Human into twelve groups. Each group would only be given the information and the Keys for the specific star gate that they were assigned to guard. This was a method for higher security. If war occurs in the future, not all the star gates would fall into the control of the enemies.

Being fully etheric, Soul Human could shape-shift at will. They did not yet have gender. They were male and female Energy in one body. To reproduce, they simply use their will power to make an extension of their entire body and pop out another Soul Human, fully adult and the exact replica of the original body.

However, if they join their energy field bodies with other nonhuman species, the result would be new mix bodies. These could be fully etheric, meaning cloud like, or semi etheric, meaning partly solid animal and partly human. The new mix creature would not have the knowledge and power of the original Soul Human. This new body could be damaged and die.

Sprkle again asked permission to be one of the Soul Human so that he could acquire a life experience on Earth. Permission was granted, and he was then prepared accordingly. When Sprkle and his group of new Soul Human first appeared on Earth, the local native dwellers were in awe to see them as they drifted gently down from the sky like illuminated clouds. It was so lovely they thought they were gods, and they worshiped them.

The new human landed on a special zone specially prepared to receive them in order to give them time to adjust to the local environment.

After a brief period of familiarization of the atmospheric condition, the Soul Humans were separated into twelve groups and sent to different corners of the planet. Each group was given special assignment. They were also expected to learn about cohabiting with other races and acquired knowledge and experiences for their own spiritual growth.

Sprkle and the rest of his group of 1,200 were assigned to live among the seashore communities. They were to guard one big star gate under the water. He was happy to be able to explore the sea. With an etheric body, he did not eat solid food. He only needed to absorb light and air to live.

Sprkle had learned that the ocean and all its creatures and landscape was modelled after the Water Kingdom of Tara, with the exception of some creatures that was more adaptable to the 3D atmosphere.

When he was in Tara, his observation of its water world was from an external view. This time he wanted to be inside the ocean, studying and learning as one of the living creature.

He would use his shape-changing ability to stay long period of time in water as various kinds of fish to facilitate his exploration.

There were underwater mountains, trees, plants of all sizes and shapes; and they were all multicoloured. Trees here were unlike those on land that had roots firmly grown into the ground. Here, they hung in mid water. The roots were free from any attachment.

The creatures of the water kingdom were so varied that Sprkle was amazed to see so many different species. He thought that there must be at least a hundred million or more. They were mostly giants. Whales were considered medium size, but there were myriads of very tiny fish.

There was a perfect feeding cycle. Plants produced food for the small fish that were in great abundance, and they in turn were food for the big fish, which had a much lower productive rate. In this way the ecosystem in the water world was in balance.

Another aspect of this world, which Sprkle found fascinating, was that everything here moved and migrated from one area to another in accordance to the sea current. Nothing in the water world ever stood still. In this seemingly silent world, Sprkle learned that lots of communication was going on between all the sea creatures and plants. It was ultrasound and even telepathy. They used them to navigate around the planet.

Here Sprkle had spent most of his time adopting bodies of different sea creatures, exploring different levels of the sea even to the abyss where no sunlight ever reached. Even in this dark area, he saw creatures were able to survive. They were smaller in size compared with the upper-level creatures. They were mostly blind and moved about with the aids of feelers. They also could generate light within their transparent bodies. Sprkle saw lighted creatures floating, swimming, and dancing in the dark, like clusters of stars. It was so wonderful to behold.

Just when Sprkle thought that he had learned everything sea-wise, he caught sight of an unusual creature. Its face and body was like a fairy with pointed ears and big round eyes, neck with gills, and very long fishtail. It was very pretty. It was golden colour or rather there was golden light shone throughout the body.

It was floating alone very calmly and happily. Sprkle looked at her and was mesmerized. Suddenly, it noticed him in the form of a giant shrimp nearby watching her with large ugly protruding eyes. She sped away very fast fearfully. Out of curiosity, Sprkle followed and down and down they went, shooting like jets deeper and deeper into the dark abyss.

Sprkle saw a flicker of light at a distance. As they approached it, the light grew bigger and soon a whole underwater city appeared in front of him. He saw that there was golden light everywhere, but he could not find the origin of this light. It looked as if this place was made up of millions of giant transparent jellyfish that were like houses encasing inside many dwellers who were difficult to define from a distance.

Sprkle stopped moving forward to observe more and saw the little fairy fish swam quickly into one of the transparent globe and there she disappeared among the same-looking creatures.

Sprkle knew that if he went in as a giant shrimp form he had adopted it would cause disturbance or even alarm, so he shape-shifted into an orb of golden light to blend in the surrounding and entered slowly into one of the globe.

He discovered that this world was immense. It was the oldest kingdom on Earth. It was created long before there was land anywhere.

There was a king and a queen and a hierarchy system. There was male and female, and they procreated by joining their bodies together when it was time to spawn. Each pair could produce hundreds of little golden eggs.

The king and queen sat at the top of the pecking order, but they were not above or better than the rest of the community. Each level of the hierarchy knew their roles and functions. Each knew their own place in the society according to the law and order of the realm.

Having learned this, Sprkle knew instantly that this ancient kingdom was the real guardian of the planet. They had been created to nourish; to monitor; to work with the wind, the air, and sunlight. And together they maintain the order of the life cycle and the balance of the ecosystem of the whole planet. They were the real guardians of underwater star gate. They were hidden deep in the abyss to be safe, to be untouchable and unreachable by any disturbing forces on the surface.

Without wanting to cause any ripple, Sprkle left quickly, changed his body into a sword fish, and sped back up to the surface homeland to jot down his findings. He silently thanked them for their quiet yet enormously grand contribution to the planet. Furthermore, he silently praised the angelic beings who created Terra for their foresight, their intelligent creation, and mostly for their deep love.

He never returned to the golden kingdom again.

Sprkle would have periodical meetings with Soul Human from other areas to exchange new learnings and experiences.

So from them he learned a little about the life on land.

In the middle land kingdom, especially the forest, there were gigantic animals. They lived mainly where there were thick foliage and trees. They were mainly vegetarian and mostly land based, but some could fly while others could swim and eat big fish. Here, elves and fairies maintain the natural ecosystem.

Skirting this area would be the different star visitors and mix races, the peaceful ones, the aggressive ones, the good and the bad ones—they were all spread out all over the land.

He learned that those more solid mix-humans would take food from the nearby trees and sometimes they would take fish. Those half-etheric race would only eat food in liquid form. As for Soul Human Race, they only took in light and air to live.

The seashore area was big enough for different races to share the natural resources; therefore, they lived in peace.

So for Srpkle, life on Tangia was mostly happy and lots of new learnings to fill his ever-growing curiosity. When he felt he had enough he transformed his Soul Human body and returned to home base as a sphere of light. There he continued his observation of Earth.

He moved the holographic record time forward. After millions of years cohabiting and interbreeding with ETs and animal races, Sprkle saw that the structure and physical form of many of the Soul Human had changed. Some new human had bird heads and human bodies, some dog bodies with human heads, others toad heads with bodies of four-legged animals, some had reptilian heads' and human bodies with reptile tails, others part horses and part apes, and so on and so forth. Only about 10 percent of the Soul Human had retained their original form and original genetic imprint. Both the Kong Yan and the Reptilian tribes were experts in genetic manipulation. They had created many different types of hybrid creatures.

Most of these creatures were used as their slaves, making weapons, and others were used as soldiers or simply as food source.

Wheels of time turned, and the population of planet Earth grew in size, and the differences among earthlings also grew, and soon Tangia seemed to be too small to satisfy the growing need of everyone. There was discontent, intolerance, then anger. Then everyone wanted more space, more this, more that, more of everything. Walls and fortresses were everywhere.

On the distant horizon an ominous black cloud was forming.

The First War on Earth

Many years passed, and Sprkle noticed that the belligerent members of the POWR Federation had become the biggest and the most dominant group in the whole Tangian population. On top of that they are constantly inviting other warring factions from nearby star clusters to bring in higher technology for weapons.

Having experienced the disaster of Tara, Sprkle was very much concerned about the future.

"Teacher, what is going on? Please explain."

And the teacher said, "Having lost the opportunity to capture the star gates in Tara and their grand galactic plan thwarted the last time, they vowed not to fail this time. The POWR Federation wanted the Healing Bridge Zone and all the star gates set on Earth, and through them they could reach any part of other galaxies in an instant."

"Thank you, Teacher, I will move time forward and see what happens." He saw that the POWR Federation had over the years been experimenting and developing all kinds of weapons of mass destruction. Their pile up now had gone so massive that they were ready to have an outright rebellion. All the while they were aided and abated by the evil power of the Dark Angels from higher dimensions.

Purple Flame further explained, "This rebellion will be against all the Divine Masters in the Celestial Realm, all the archangels and angels from 12D all the way down to 2D. They were going to have an outright war to establish their Dark Empire on all levels of the whole universe.

"They did not want to be monitored, they did not want to follow the Law of the Universe as established by the Masters of Light, they did not want rules and regulations, they did not want emotion, and they did not want to love or to be loved. For this freedom they will fight and destroy any force that was put in their way.

"However, their vibrational power could not go beyond the tenth dimension because that was where they cut off from God by creating a solid permanent shield from that energy.

"The Celestial Elder and the Galactic Guardian Angels were aware of the flow of things happening with the Federation, and they issued a stern warning to stop the war plan.

"Meanwhile, on the other hand, they were also preparing contingency measures. They assembled the Angelic Rescue Team once again, and also Light Warriors were called in from different dimensions and universes. They knew that the Dark Angels are also Archangels themselves, and they were formidable foe.

"On the Light Warriors side, they also had advance weapon enough to meet any threat and also the advantage of having divine support from the highest universal realm, the Titanic Power of Rishi, which create and run cosmoses. And they were monitoring this drama as it unfolds without interfering for the moment."

Sprkle observed that the Galactic Council of Peace tried to conduct diplomatic discussions with the POWR Federation in the hope to avoid further conflicts. Then after a short stalemate period, the negotiation for peace was thrown out and the war of wars began.

Star Wars

This war was the first on planet Earth, but they were fought on all fronts of the Milky Way galaxy and on every dimensions as high as the tenth. These kind of wars were fought with electric lightning bolts, laser shots, nuclear, sound waves, and many other super weapons that caused widespread and unimaginable catastrophe.

During these wars, billions of spaceships of all sizes and shapes zigzag in all corners of space. Every dimension could not escape the bolts of lightning. The myriads of laser beam and saser waves cross fires everywhere. Planets, stars, asteroids and anything that was touched would explode instantly and turned into space dust, electric lightning rods, like gigantic spider webs speeding across the skies, burning and exploding everything in their ways.

Sprkle was horrified, as he watched this vast scale cataclysm on the holographic screen.

Unfortunately, the little fragile planet Earth was reluctantly drawn into the war mainly because the Bridge Zone was set up in the vicinity and all the star gates were in full operation. Sprkle quickly zoomed into Earth to see what happened to her. He was most concerned.

He saw thousands of spaceships hovering in the Earth's sky. Then without warning of any kind, deadly laser beams shot out from hundreds of them, and then on the other side of the sky, another type of spacecrafts returned shots. And soon fire and explosions were everywhere in the sky and on the ground.

Suddenly, there were very bright beams of unusual lights beating on Earth's surface, and then her electric and magnetic grid was disturbed. This grid was her lifeline that fed energy all around the globe. Next, her core centre energy was not functioning properly, and tremendous heat was building up very quickly. The next thing that happened was a massive explosion at the centre followed by series of smaller explosions occurred simultaneously around the whole planet.

Earth's grid was severely damaged, followed by leakage of energy, then followed by the loss of thrust to spin. Then she wobbled, and her axis tilted. She was severely crippled.

Sprkle in panic called out to Purple Flame, who appeared immediately and said to him, "Earth would have been totally destroyed if at this point in time the Titanic Masters of the Rishi Universe did not intervene. They sent down the Titanic Warriors of the twelfth dimensions, who overpowered the enemies. They saved Earth in the nick of time, but this multidimensional star war went on nonstop for over nine hundred years." Here Sprkle could not help, but ask this question: "Why the Titanic Masters of Light did not intervene earlier? Why did Earth had to suffer so?" The ever-patient Purple Flame explained, "Before the creation of this solar system, it had been decided that this would be a special experimental project where it would be left to develop totally on its own natural way. This means everything here that has life and consciousness will be given freedom of choice. They are constantly monitored and watched over by angelic guardians, who could assist and guide but not interfere.

"Free will was given as a gift, and with it, the planets and their inhabitants could choose their own mode of action. Only—and I repeat, only—when the scale of balance is tipped so badly that the situation may have detrimental effect on whole galaxy, then the Higher Masters would exercise their privilege to override the free will agreement and to stop further destruction. What you had witnessed was just that."

"Moreover, the Free Will Agreement has the advantage of allowing evolution to expand in a more diverse manner than if they were managed and controlled by the Galactic Council. We have seen life developed into new and unexpected ways that we have not seen before in the universe. Therefore, it is not a bad thing. You continue to look and learn, my dear." And so with a heavy heart Sprkle saw that for four thousand years Earth could not sustain physical life. Everything that could die were turned into dust and buried. She was plagued with constant land eruptions, volcanic outbursts, manic storms, other weird weather patterns, and so forth. The water world that Sprkle loved so much experienced boiling temperature, and everything in it turned into mush.

As if all these were not enough, the breaking up of the global energy grid also tore apart the one and only land mass. Big chunks of the land drifted apart from each other, and floods filled the gaps.

From then on Tangia was no more.

Watching this horrible, nightmarish disaster unfold before his tender eyes, Sprkle broke down in tears and grief. This was too much to bear. He screamed in desperation and pain.

Seeing this, Purple Flame knew that this meant spiritual growth of his beloved young student. At first Sprkle was inconsolable. He gave him time to let out his deep painful feelings and then wrapped him around with this warm loving energy to bring him back to a more balanced state of mind. He said, "Being a witness to this kind of destruction and evil serves as soul lessons. This shows that life in the universe is not only the wonderful world of the angelic realm that you are used to. One must see the different aspects of life and then learn in order to grow in wisdom. Emotional joy and pain is part of the lessons in the Book of Life."

Sprkle took some time to recover his emotional state and continued to watch the drama in the Book of Records. He thought that he was fortunate that he was not caught in the crossfire this time.

He was safe because, unlike the catastrophe of Tara, which happened suddenly, this Star Wars was years in the making; therefore, there was time for evacuation to take place for those who wished to leave the planet. They were brought by spaceships to a nearby peaceful planet. Once arrived, they were brought into the underground caves, which were big enough to accommodate hundreds of cities. They were told that when the time was ripe they would be brought back to Earth.

The Cave Dwellers

Sprkle wanted to experience life in the underground. He changed the frequency of his soul body, and with the aid of an angel, he was human again. He stayed with the rest of the refugees and took time to explore the area.

He saw that when they arrived, there were other cave dwellers. Some were human, and some were not. But they were set apart from others so that they could take their time to re-establish their lives in the new environment. He saw that their parts of the caves were already well prepared to receive them. There were clear waterfalls, rivers, trees with fruits and other plants, and all other basic necessities for their survival.

The underground was a world not very different from the surface. There was light albeit dimmer than the sunlight. There were very big and tall buildings enough to house thousands of human beings. There were entrances and exits big enough for spaceships and shuttles to go through. He also found out that apart from the human beings there were other star travellers and creatures each tribe living in their specific quarters. These dwellers had been living in this area for millions of years before his arrival.

After spending some years in this world, Sprkle returned to home base to further investigate the rescue work of the planet.

The Galactic Council ordered another Rescue Team to control damage and repair the planetary grid and set the planet spinning again albeit at different frequency and rhythm because of the tilt. Rather than causing more destruction if the planet was to be moved back to its original position, the Rescue Team decided to let things stand for the time being.

The Soul Human and other races who had full etheric body structure did not perish like the rest of the creatures.

Full etheric beings were simply energy; therefore, they could change form, but they do not die.

All other ETs, mixed human/animals, dinosaurs, and other creatures that remained on the land all perished.

The Bridge Zone was destroyed, and some of the star gates that were captured by the enemies were either damaged or closed, and their guardians were evacuated to a safe place to be replaced by Angelic Warriors. Soul Human assignment was a peaceful one only.

Ice Age set in, and the whole planet Earth was frozen for millions of years.

In order to prevent more invasions from other worlds and also give space and time for Mother Earth to heal, the Damage Control Angels spread an electromagnetic fence around the whole planet and put Earth in quarantine. This meant that nothing could come in or go out beyond the third dimension. This was called the Seal.

The series of explosions on Earth sent shockwaves all around the neighbouring star systems and far beyond. Therefore, fencing the whole globe meant that whatever happened in and around this planet the effect could not contaminate other systems and their inhabitants.

From then on Earth was officially a prison planet.

CHAPTER 3

THE PRISON PLANET

The Aftermath

Right after the Star Wars, the once young, vibrant, blue planet Earth was in a state of ruins. Destruction was vast, deep, and everywhere.

The once single land mass, Tangia, was torn into pieces, cut through like knife in butter by earthquakes. Water filled in the gaps, separating each land fragments and pushing them further apart from each other. Some smaller pieces sank into the ocean, which became a death trap for all life with its hot steaming water. Earth itself was crippled with a tilted axis.

Earth would have been totally destroyed if not for the intervention of the Titanic Master of Light, which ended the conflict just in time. Amid all the chaos, this particular planet cannot be allowed to end. It was decided by the Galactic Council.

Earth was created, nourished, given life and human beings, and assisted to evolve to a higher vibration. The Bridge Zone and multidimensional portals and star gates were installed here because of the original plan of full integration of Terra, Tara, and Gaia.

But now most of her life-forms were wiped out, and she was under a thick cover of ice.

Sprkle moved time a couple of millions of years ahead, and he saw that Earth's grid was repaired. Her weather condition, even though not like before, at least, was stable and the sea temperature was brought down to life sustaining level. Instead of one land, there are many lands, and the one big ocean of before was now many seas skirting the big lands and millions of islands scattered everywhere.

He also observed that the weather pattern has changed. The tilt of the Earth's axis meant that the sun rises and sets at different parts of the planet, and now she has seasons. This also meant that the season on the Northern Hemisphere is opposite to the season on the Southern Hemisphere.

This time around Sprkle saw an abundant new life-forms and bigger varieties than ever before. The seasons had changed everything. Sprkle was excited.

Sprkle asked, "Teacher, is this time for me to have a new adventure?" Purple Flame cautioned, "No, not yet. This is too early yet. When the land movement has slow down, the weather pattern stable. The Angelic Guardian are monitoring and helping to speed up the healing process. I will let you know when it will be time for you to go."

Purple flame pointed to one specific area of the holographic worlds and said, "My dear, you can focus your attention to here, and you will see the further development of the Earth's history."

Further observation had revealed to Sprkle more disaster on a deeper level, on the soul level. Here he needed explanations.

He asked, "Teacher what happened to the souls after Earth was quarantined?"

Purple Flame explained, "Earthlings were semi etheric and some fully etheric in their form, but no matter what structures their body, they all had either group soul identity or single unit soul identity, but they all had souls. "All souls carried the Divine Spark of Light of God, and with that they all needed to go through the ascension process to return to God no matter which level of dimension they are at. If they have incarnated to the 3D level after death, they should move up to 4D and climb the 'ladder' of ascension one step at a time until they reach the highest rung to reunite with the Source, the Original Creator of all Life. This is the Law of the Universe, which I had explained to you before.

"The Seal had caused a major problem for the souls on Earth. You know that every creature on Earth is intrinsically linked with the planet through its Personal Energy Field no matter one is animal or human. And so when the Seal was set for the whole planet it was also set inside the Personal Energy Field of each and every creature living on the planet. This means that every soul will carry its individual Seal until the Planetary Seal is lifted off.

"That means those who died in the 2D level because of the Seal could only reincarnate back to 2D, and those of 3D could only incarnate to 3D. This state of affair would remain until the Seal was taken off. The planet is a prison, and all souls its prisoners. Since Soul Human and other etheric race could not die, they were trapped within the 4D world. The only way out was to reincarnate to the 3D or lower dimensions. From then on, evolution of souls on Earth had stopped. On top of that there was also another problem that was not foreseen before and that is amnesia.

"Trapped souls who reincarnate, whether on 3D or lower levels, are all born with total memory loss. They cannot remember the wars, their connection with their spirit. They developed tunnel vision and lost awareness of the presence of God's loving spirit of Light within their very own soul. They have lost sight of this.

"Sprkle, you do not need to be disheartened, I can see your energy field is shrinking. Do not worry because this is not permanent. The Seal will be taken off in time when the condition is safe to do so. Remember, the Seal was set up to protect the planet in the first place."

Patiently, Sprkle moved time forward a million years, and indeed he saw that a new dimensional portal and Bridge Zone was set up between Earth, the 4D transition point, and one additional bridge and portal linked with a star, Sirius B.

With the Seal still in place for the planet, the trapped and contaminated souls could be brought to 4D through the portals, then to Sirius B to be healed. Here their individual Seal that was set there after the Star Wars could be taken off.

Sprkle felt joy and hope. He could hardly wait for the new human race seeding so that he could jump back to Earth for another round.

By this time all the sea creatures were reintroduced; and the condition on land were covered with trees, foliage, flora and fauna. There were mountains and rivers and many volcanoes, which erupted often to create even more new land.

There were new land animals on the continents and on the islands.

The condition to introduce higher intelligent species was ripe.

This time the semi etheric animal beings were allowed to gradually move toward a more solid human form. In time, with genetic mutations, even some of the apes were walking upright. This race would eventually split from the animal ape species all together and became new human race. This race would be called Earth Seeds. They still had a very animalistic and primitive mind. Their lifestyle was not very different from the apes.

New Human-The Earth Seed Human and Star Seed Human

After millions of years Sprkle noticed that the genetic structure and the formation of many of the Soul Human had changed.

With the help of the Angelic New Life Team, physical human beings were created in adult form and equipped with all the proper organs for procreation. They were created in the fourth dimension.

These were Star Seed Human. They were the descendants of the first Astral Human Race. Their genetic imprints in their soul body were those from the original Tarancodes. They also had genes from Sirius B race and Angelic Blue Race from higher realm; therefore, they had a twelve- dimensional power. Their physical bodies were immortal. When they wanted to end a life journey, they simply walked into another dimension, adopted a new physical body, and continued living.

This time they were male and female with equal standing. They were paired one male and one female as one family. Then they put twelve families as one tribe and each tribe with a different skin pigment.

They became the brown race, the red race, the black race, the yellow race, and the white race.

The colour was only on skin level; underneath they were all the same.

Each colour race was dispatched to different parts of the planet with all the basic elements and conditions so that they may survive and evolve according to their surrounding resources.

Thousands of years passed, and the Star Seed Human population grew very quickly. In time they became two subrace, and they were called the Lamanian and Alanian.

They lived in different part of the planet: some in the cold region, some in the hot tropical region, and others lived somewhere in between, the more temperate zones. They lived according to the natural resources in their surroundings. They lived on mountain areas, some on the valleys, some near the sea, some in caves, and even in the underworlds.

Both the Lamanian and Alanian were highly intelligent, and so wherever they were, they would create a culture of high learnings, equality for all people, lived harmoniously with nature and their neighbours. They introduced good governance.

They lived apart from the Earth Seed Human, who chose to live closer to their ape ancestors in the woods and jungle areas. Whenever they needed help, Star Seed Human would teach them new ways, like the creation of fire to keep warm and ward off harmful creatures. Also they introduced farming when they were ready to change from hunting. Some adopted new ways and others remained the same.

Gradually the Earth Seed Human interbred with some of the Star Seed Human. After many generations, the Earth/Star Seeds' new breeds were less animal like and adopted a different lifestyle. This group evolved very slowly. After millions of years, they practically did not change much, and even though they walked upright and their arms shorter than those of apes, their level of intelligence was still very low.

Peace prevailed on Earth for thousands of years. In view of this, the Galactic Guardian lifted the Seal and thereafter the star gates were fully functional for interstellar travel again.

Moreover, with the lifting of the Seal, ascension for the souls of both Alanian and Lamanians were possible.

The Dracos

During the period of peace time, those reptile/human who were allowed to reincarnate to third and second dimensions were transforming into human form as they absorbed more and more human genes with every passing generation. But they were the descendants of the Dracos race, and so their aggressive and cold-blooded reptilian traits remained.

And so peace did not last long before this group started to amass power and weapons to terrorize other communities. In time they infiltrated the high genetic codes of the Lamanian and Alanian race by interbreeding with them.

The situation had gone so far that the Angelic Council saw that they needed to intervene. The original Tara Astral Human Star Seed bloodline could not be allowed to fully corrupt.

Angered by this intervention, the Dracos waged war.

Once again the Angel Warriors of Light were being called up to defend.

The Light Warriors managed to overpower the Dracos by shutting down their main control system and by throwing a high frequency band of sound and energy net all over their lairs, a frequency too high for the Dracos to penetrate, and they surrendered. They were sent to exile in another prison planet far away.

However, not all left, the mix-blood children Dracon/Human race remained on Earth. These and other Lamanians and Alanians went underground world to escape the war on the surface.

The Draco war damaged the Earth's electromagnetic grid, which led to widespread earth movements, causing volcanic eruptions everywhere. Black smoke and dust shot up hundreds of miles up into the Earth stratosphere, and black rain poured down for forty days and forty nights. The sun was shut off, and again ice age came, and Mother Earth was still for the next 6,500 years.

The Nephilin

Again Sprkle moved the wheel of time forward to about 950,000 BCE, and he observed that the planetary condition was again brought to bear new seeding of life.

This time he saw a new race of human. They were called the Nephilin. They were a hybrid created between the Dark Angels and a human race called the Annunak. They were giants, both male and female.

Since they carried the genetic imprint of the Fallen Dark Angels of the tenth dimension; therefore, they were Star Seed. Being driven by their self-serving power, the Nephilin were elitist, aggressive, and ruthless.

They were huge, average about fifteen to twenty feet tall, both male and female and therefore needed to consume a lot of food. They liked to eat meat, and often they would eat any kinds of animals that were in their vicinity, and when there was not enough they would eat human, their slaves.

They had no respect for the natural world around them. They would often wage war against their own species, kill them, and eat them; or they would capture them as slaves.

Everywhere these giants went they would devour everything and leave behind barren land soiled with blood and decay.

Many times the Angelic Council sent emissaries to try to bring balance to the destruction by helping the rest of the population to defend themselves and sometimes raise revolts and even war against the giants. Some communities built high walls as a deterrent against the giants, and these did not always work. Fights and conflicts occurred frequently as the giants were always advancing in all directions in conquests and in search for more slaves. This went on for about fifty thousand years.

In view of this abuse of power, the Angelic Council and the Galactic Guardian devised a plan to stop the Nephilin. They could clearly see that the rest of the races, be it animal or human, were no match to them and that they could see clearly that if left unaided the ending would be bad indeed. There was an urgent need for balance here.

They then created another hybrid race with the gift of superior power and genetic codes. This was the SERRES. This race was aligned with the higher avatar level at the eleventh dimension, therefore more intelligent and more powerful than the Nephilin.

The SERRES were godlike in nature. They carried around them a high vibration and light. They were both very advance in science and technology as well as in all aspects of spiritual matter.

They were master of energy field manipulation, and they could create from cellular level any matter they want, from food source to even spaceships.

They were assigned to be the guardian of all the dimensional portals and interstellar star gates on Earth and also to stop the Nephilin from tipping the scale.

The Nephilin needed permission from the SERRES to go through each star gates each time they wanted to exit. They were furious that they were constantly policed by this new breed of beings. This condition was not acceptable by them. They were very angry to be subjected to such kind of humiliation. They hated the idea of having to deal with a race of human who had the potential to destroy them.

Sprkle moved time forward to an important day and was shocked to see a full-blown war was going on. On one side were the Nephilin, plus the members of the POWR Federation, which included the Draco/human, the Annunaks, the reptilians, and so forth. This new unholy alliance had established a huge military base in Maldack and Mars.

On the other side, the SERRES, plus the Galactic Guardian Alliance of the Brotherhood of Light from the twelfth dimension, that were determined to stop the Dark Force from taking over everything.

This war was the Battle of the Giants fought with the highest ferocity on many dimensions. Eventually, just like before, the Power of Light overpowered the Federation by zapping the core centre of the Maldack planet, obliterating it into zillions of fragments, which in time formed a dead ring spinning quietly between Jupiter and Mars.

As for Mars, everything was raised to the ground with nuclear power and it became a dead planet covered with poisonous radiation.

This war lasted for 1,200 years.

Before and during the war most human and animals were evacuated to other more peaceful star systems nearby, namely to Arcturus, Alcion, and also Sirius.

Then came yet another periodic poles shift on Earth, which resulted in another ice age from 956,500 to 950,000 BCE.

Time Forward to about 800,000 BCE – The Urtite

Peace time again. Sprkle noticed that after each ice age the planet's landscape change quite drastically. The land and sea were moved by the ice sheets and the subsequent deluge. What was on the east moved to the west and what was on the north moved to the south and so forth.

Sprkle thought he was seeing a totally new planet.

Not only the total landscape had changed, even the new breed of plants and animals were also different.

A new breed of human appeared on Earth.

They were called the Urtite. They were the result of interbreeding between the Lamanians, who survived the last war and returned to the surface from the underground, and the SERRES who returned from exile. And so this new race of human beings were descendants of the unbroken lineage of the original Angelic Astral Human.

By this time, even though there was peace, most of the land and sea were still contaminated by the nuclear radiation left over by the previous war. And so the Urtite and many surface refugees of different species lived primarily underground.

The Urtite were learned people with knowledge of high spiritual values. They developed a sophisticated civilization in the Inner Earth.

They were assigned as guardians of an important dimensional portals there.

They reintroduced the ancient teachings of the power of Divine Love and the Law of the Universe. They established the school for training teachers and priesthood. They were known as the Priest of Ur.

Sprkle asked permission to reincarnate as an Urtite student to learn more. Permission was granted. He did not want to be born as a baby, and so arrangement was made for him to adopt an adult physical male body. He chose to be a thirteen-year-old boy, and he was brought by an angel to the school for his first initiation.

Sprkle found that unlike the underground cave world that he had experienced before, which catered mainly to a survival mode of living, yet this new Earth's inner world was exquisite, this was created with higher ideals in mind.

He was first brought to the temple for higher knowledge, where all the students and teachers lived.

There was one building for living and another huge building with wide open space and many chambers was for teaching. Each chamber was very big and contained all the necessary devices and equipment of most advance technology. The books, scrolls, and reading materials covered all the walls. There was hall for art, hall for science, hall for philosophy, hall for astrology, hall for sound and music, hall for advance spiritual studies and experimentations, and so forth. There was knowledge and information available to cater for every hungry mind.

After a brief tour of the temple and school, standing among the lush green rolling hills dotted with colourful flowers, Sprkle thought he had gone to heaven. It was here and nowhere else on Earth that had all the elements to satisfy his insatiable curious mind. He wanted to know EVERYTHING.

Sprkle learned about the Law of the Universe;
the basic law of creation;
life force energy, vibration, frequencies and movement;
sound and colours;
electromagnetic force;
how to build with the electromagnetic force;
how to create with sound, colour, and frequencies;
how to create force field;
learned about geometrical symbols;
how to use symbols as keys to open and change forms; and
how to use the mind to levitate, to time travel, to create and change
objects and so forth.

Whenever he had spare time, he would travel out of the school and
explore the underground world. It was indeed a massive world. Sprkle
saw rivers, lakes, forests, even mountains and valleys. There were all the
flora and fauna that one could find on the surface before.

He also discovered that the Urtite race was not the only dwellers in
the underworld. There were many other races from different star systems
and cultures occupying different areas. They were already there since the
first star war, and they never left. They were the ancient builders of the
first underworld civilization.

There were flying vehicles of different sizes and shapes. One thing
that amazed Sprkle was that he could see the sky and also stars. There
were huge hangers for parking spaceships and star cruisers. This he did
not expect.

Well, Sprkle thought, *life here is just great. Who could ask for anything
more?*

Time passed and Sprkle lived here for many, many years.

When the condition on the surface was liveable again, some of the
Urtites gradually went up to the surface and helped with the rebuilding.
Together with other human beings, they built villages, then towns and
later cities. Sprkle was very much involved in the work, and he enjoyed
every minute of it.

When he was too old to work, he discarded the old body and
went to the fourth dimension to adopt a new body and continued
living among the Urtite race, sometimes as student and sometimes as

teacher. Eventually he was promoted to be one of the high priest of Ur. He reincarnated many times, always travelling and teaching until Earth condition changed again. For hundreds of thousands of years, the Urtites worked to raise the evolution of humanity through introducing new knowledge, advance technology, and the art of living harmoniously with others. In time they expanded their influence to many parts of the planet: to East Asia, North and South America, central Europe, Egypt, and the other middle Eastern areas. Everywhere they went, they built temples and halls for learning.

Under the Urtite beings, Earth had enjoyed one of the highest level of civilized culture, the golden age of art, and peaceful creativity.

One fine day Sprkle thought it was time to return to home base and to continue his observation of the history from a higher perspective.

Nibiru and the Nibiruan

It was 450,000 BCE, and Sprkle saw a planet approaching Earth. It was Nibiru, the last planet of the solar system. Its very elliptical orbit brought it either too far away from the sun, its coldest time, and or nearest to the sun, their hottest time.

In order for the planet and its dwellers to survive this extreme condition the Nibiruan created a special atmospheric blanket around the planet so that their temperature remains at a constant comfortable level. One of the crucial element for this special "blanket" is pulverised gold.

Having learned about this from the holographic scanner, Sprkle zoomed closer and saw three huge spaceships came out of the planet and flew closer to Earth and then he saw three smaller shuttles flew out of one of the mother ship and landed at the edge a river somewhere in the Middle East.

Sprkle wondered what they were doing. He then zoomed into one of the ship's exploration scanning system and found out that they were looking for gold. Their plan was to mine it and bring home as much gold dust as they could before the home planet swing off to the far distance again.

Next he saw some human-looking beings came out of one small ship. They were carrying equipment to test the ground and dirt. After a while more shuttles came with people and they started to work on the ground. Sprkle then zoomed into their mother ship to look for their leader.

He saw a big male figure, giving orders and monitoring everything. He was very tall, big bright eyes, long braided golden hair. He was highly intelligent, and he had a sort of aura of light around him. He looked like an embodiment of power. Obviously, he was the leader of the mining operation.

Sprkle was curious about the Nibiruan. He found out that on their planet there were two races. There was those of the royal lineage, possessing semi etheric bodies, could shift shape at will, highly intelligent, and expert of genetic engineering and matters of light. Then there was the other race, who also looked like human, but they seemed to be a weaker and lower caste. These were the working caste, almost like slaves.

The royal Nibiruan were elitist, behaved like demigods. Even though they were not as aggressive as the Kong Yan, they were ruthless and self- serving. They also possess very advance war weapons and ready to use them.

After seeing this, Sprkle turned his attention back to Earth and moved time forward a few hundred years. He saw huge mining installations spreading all over Africa from north to south and other parts of the globe. The operation was going on full throttle with hundreds of Nibiruan busy at extraction.

Where the leaders and their families dwell, there were beautiful grand palaces and gardens usually on top of hills in the vicinity of their mines. Time passed, and Sprkle was surprised to see their next stage of development was something quite unexpected. The Nibiruan had single handily created a new race of human.

Reason? For this Sprkle turned back the time a bit and found that the Nibiruan workers were dying very quickly due to their physical structure not suitable for long stay in Earth's dense atmosphere. There were sporadic mutinies, which affected the mining operation.

The royal family needed to solve this problem quickly. Being expert genetic engineers who created their own slave caste, this time they are going to create a new slave race to ensure their long-term project will not stop.

Having learned the reason, Sprkle moved time forward and saw that this new Slave Race Human was actually mutated Earth Seed

Human race. They were about seven feet tall, very muscular torsos and limbs. They looked like straight walking apes with less body hair. They were given low-level intelligence so that they would be easy to control. The Niburian called them sheep and their gods the shepherds.

In the beginning there were only men, later they also introduced female to ensure the slave bloodline continue.

And so for thousands of years the Nibiruan settled in the Middle East area, then Africa, and later expanded also to North and South America and other parts of Earth where there were gold to be found and created more slave human hybrids along the way.

Except for occasional battles among the royal family members, the mining operation was going well until one day the leader saw on their holographic scanner the possibility of another Earth's periodical climate change. This meant it was time to pack up and leave, but before they depart, they properly stored up the genetic elements of the slave race and some useful animals from Earth for later use.

They left, but they will be back.

Soon the sky opened, and rain poured down, covering the surface of Earth from pole to pole, and she rested.

AFTER THE GLOBAL DELUGE

Sprkle turned the Akashic time clock to 75,000 BCE. The flood water receded; and once again, after many years, Earth surface was restored to her former life-giving self. New landscape and weather patterns. New plants, animals, and sea life.

Watching this picture on the holographic screen, Sprkle was amazed at the power, the stamina, and resilience of Mother Earth.

He said, "Mother Earth, you are a great survivor. I love you."

Mua

Sprkle noticed that there were two additional huge land mass, two continents each on opposite side of the globe.

One big continent was called Mua. He saw that there were many different communities living in different hubs in the north, south, east, and west of the big land; and they were so far apart from each other that they were not aware of each other's existence.

There were farmers, hunters, gatherers. Different community lived according to the weather condition and the natural resources available to them in their hub area.

Sprkle observed that this land was known as the Empire of the Sun. On the edge of the land, one can see the first rising of the sun. Their numerology number was three. Their crown symbol was three peaks with three points in a row. Their language was mostly hieroglyphics.

Those in the north, people lived in temperate weather condition. Their plant and animal species were different from those of the south. Even the skin texture and colour of the people was also different. The northerners have lighter skin, and the southerners had mainly darker or tan colour skin. Majority of the Mua population on the whole had black hair.

The southern part of Mua was a tropical paradise: big forest and rich agriculture. The general landscape was mountainous, mostly volcanic, which provided the land with very fertile soil. Trees and plants here were gigantic. It had a long coastline and golden beaches. The sea was big, powerful and teamed with fantastic and colourful sea life.

Sprkle felt that he would like to reincarnate again and experience a new journey in the land of Mua. He called up his loving teacher Purple Flame, who appeared instantly.

Sprkle asked, "Teacher, can I try another round of reincarnation on this beautiful place? But this time I want to be a tree. I had been a giant shrimp living in the sea before, so this time I think it would be nice to live as a tree. I wonder what it would be like to live as a banana tree. Can I do that?"

Purple Flames knows him too well. Sprkle's curiosity is unstoppable. He wants to learn *everything*.

"Ha-ha. Of course, my dear. You sure you do not want to be a snail first? All right, you have permission to go. How about right now?"

Sprkle's mind went blank for a moment. Next thing he knew, his consciousness woke up and he saw darkness around him. After a while he realized that he was a seed buried in the ground. He waited—there was nothing else to do.

One day he felt he had more strength and he could move. He wanted to crack open the shell, and by sheer magic the coat that surrounded him for so long peeled off, and he was free. He saw himself as a tiny green shoot with a strong desire to move up. There was only one direction as far as he was concerned, and that was to move up and to reach for the sunlight. Time passed, and Sprkle was a young shoot out of the dark soil and bathing in the daily sunlight, which was vital for his survival. He saw that his plant body was moving in two directions, one up and one down.

He was developing roots, which was moving into the ground deeper and deeper, and the other part of him was going up and up every day.

He had no concern about anything else if not the daily shower from the sky and the light, which was important for his body to grow.

Days gone by, then months came and gone, and one day Sprkle looked at his body, and it was fully grown banana tree. He liked his branches and huge leaves swaying gently in the wind like dancing fans. He was home for ants and other friendly insects. Sometimes birds came to nibble on him. What he liked best was the big bunches of bananas that hung all around him. Those were his babies. His children were many, and he was happy. He was also happy when they turned from green to yellow, a sign of maturity. People came to collect them, and they use them as food to nourish their children. Seeing this, Sprkle felt a sense of fulfilment.

After several cycles of banana bearing, he felt it was time to go back to home base and perhaps try another life journey.

He thanked the tree for the precious opportunity for learning. His consciousness left the tree, which continued to live and produced bananas for years to come.

His mind went blank, and his consciousness was again on home base. He continued to monitor Mua and decided to try another experience there.

Purple Flame came and said, "Well, well, what next?"

Sprkle said, "I want to be a woman this time. I have noticed that there was a group of highly spiritual women who were called shaman, and they were the healers. Since my last reincarnation as an Urtite priest, I think I have enough knowledge to contribute to the healing work there. What do you think, my teacher? Besides, after the experience of having banana babies, it got me thinking what would it be like to be a human bearing human babies? Have you tried that before, Teacher?"

Purple Flame took a moment to tune into his very big memory bank and replied, "Yes, of course, I had. You must know that in order to qualify to be a spiritual guide and teacher, one must have gone through many different aspects of life in general. One cannot learn only from books. It is only through experiences that one really learns and the knowledge registered into the soul crystal memory, which will remain and grow as the soul evolve. The more varied the experiences, the better.

"Sprkle, the universe is at your disposal, you need only to ask. Yes, go be a woman and learn everything you can about what is the meaning to be a female human being. I am sure you will find this journey very different from everything else that you have gone through so far. One word of caution—it is quite challenging. Are you sure?"

"Yes, please."

"Then I will have to ask for permission and make the necessary arrangements. Maybe this time you start as a baby girl born and raised in the southern Mua community. This will give you a full life journey. Would you like that?"

"Yes, please," Sprkled replied enthusiastically. Not long passed, and Purple Flame reappeared.

"Now arrangement has been made for you to be born to a young female. Her name would be Naya. You would be her firstborn. You will have a young father called A'Hu. This would be a simple family, modest hut house with a patch of farm land and some goats in a rural village. Your mother would be a highly sensitive and spiritual woman. She is a shaman and herbal healer. She is very popular and very much respected by the local villagers.

"Your life-line would be a girl first educated by your mother and then later would be sent to special training school in a bigger town. This school is very exclusive. They only accept children with special talent and the highest mark for spiritual sensibility. In any case your soul memory of the Urtite knowledge would suffice to pass the initiation test. You will be a healer in this lifetime.

"When you reach the marital age of seventeen, your parents will find a husband for you. Thereafter, you will have children and raise a family. You would live to ninety years of age. You will see grandchildren. Any question?"

"Would I be able to communicate with you whenever I need?"

"Pay attention to your dreams. I shall come through there. Are you ready to go?"

"Yes."

Sprkle's mind went blank, and the next thing he knew he was a foetus in a womb. Sprkle knew how to raise his soul body and consciousness out of the unborn baby. He hovered above the pregnant female carrying the baby. He knew that he could enter the baby's body any time he wished. From the condition of the womb he learned that the baby would be born in a couple of days. Right now baby was sleeping warmly inside the mother.

Sprkle's soul flew high up in the air and hovered above the land area where he will call home. He saw that the land was rich with vegetation, the surrounding sea teamed with sea life of all kinds. The people were brown skinned and had long wavy black hair.

Male and female had equal social standing, each had their specialized area of work and responsibilities. They were peaceful and very spiritually inclined. Most of the spiritual ceremonies were conducted by women, and men were assigned to physical work. They lived with respect to the surrounding natural world. They sang songs to communicate with nature and High Spirits. They were fully God-aware people. This race of human was called the Lemurian.

This was the latest paradise, another angelic gift to Earth. Benevolent beings would come visit with their spaceships. They built energy healing posts and set up energy and light grids to heal and strengthen the planet. They did this by using specific sound waves and frequencies to move huge pieces of crystalline stones from distant quarries and set them deep into the land. Some of these grids were straight lines and others in circles.

These benevolent beings were mostly from the Sirius B star system and also from Arcturus star systems. They were also known as the Watchers to monitor Earth's progress in the evolution program.

Soon it was time to return to the womb and get ready to be born. The big moment came, and the new baby girl by the name of Amaya came to the happy embrace of Naya and A'Hu.

Baby Amaya had tan skin and big brown eyes. Her mother loved her and gave her all the proper nourishments for healthy growth. Naya often sing to the baby, and after work A'Hua would come home and bring the baby out to the nearby wood to play.

Soon it was Amaya seventh birthday, and on this day there was a simple ritual where Naya would perform a spiritual song to ask for blessings and well-being for the child and also ask for guidance that she may be taught the spiritual healing way from this day forth.

On the very next day Naya brought her daughter to a long walk along the surrounding hills where there were lots of bushes and flowers and mushrooms of different kinds. There the first lesson would be to identify what was good to consume, what was poisonous, and what was used for different healing.

Everyday Amaya would be walking and picking up plants and learning. She thought that her mother was the most knowledgeable person in the whole world.

In the beginning Naya would accompanied her to do the healing work, but as she became more efficient at most common ailments, she was allowed to practice alone. She would visit local and even far-off villages. And so mother and daughter were soon well-known and respected by grateful people whose ailments and sufferings had been eased by their caring touches. Sometimes they even saved lives.

Meanwhile, Naya also taught her daughter how to sing the spiritual way. She would teach her the proper tone to hum to invoke the High Spirit. There were ways of humming and also other sounds that could travel for many miles in all direction.

There was also healing tones for different ailments to work together with the herbal medicine.

So the daily routine for young Amaya was to wake up just before sunrise, go outdoor facing east, and sing the spiritual song to honour the sun and Mother Nature. After breakfast she and mother would go to the hills to collect herbal plants and also nuts and mushrooms. Following that, they would return home and start making medicine.

Afternoon would be spent visiting the lonely and the sick people. When that was finished, it was time to prepare dinner and that was also time when father come home from work. Life was mainly routine.

However, every year there would be celebration during the solstices and the equinoxes. During these special occasions, all the villagers would gather in a big open plain space with many big stones standing in a circle. There would be singing, music, bon fire, plenty of food. People would be sharing stories and laughter. Children would be playing games and making artwork and wreaths with all kinds of colourful flowers.

At dawn everyone would be silent, and only one person would start a solemn tune. When the first light of the sun appeared, all the people, hundreds of them, will sing as one voice—a tribute to the sun and High Spirit. It was a divine moment.

This wonderful and magical occasions would remain in Amaya's memory for a long time.

Years passed by so quickly, and one day Amaya was already twelve years old. This day Naya put some clean clothes in a small bag for her daughter and prepared some bread and cheese for a journey. It was time to leave home for further training in the town school.

It was the social rule at the time that all boys and girls must attend the government school for their vocational training to prepare them for their future professional role in the society.

Boys would be sent to school to learn about physical work, hunting, farming, and also the technique of fighting with and without weapon. Some would be sent to military school to learn about the whole range of weapons and how to use them. This kind of training was only reserve for those who had past the hardest physical tests. These would be the elite military men.

As for the girls there would be tests of sensibility and feminine intuition and so forth. There would be training for home design; caring for children, especially to be foster parents for orphans; weaving and clothe production; and art work of all types for those with ordinary pass marks.

There was a special school for the higher spiritually sensitive, and this was where Amaya was sent to study. One would only be admitted after the most rigorous of tests. There will be four years of training, and thereafter, it will be a lifetime vocational work.

There was teaching about vibration and frequencies and how to raise them, dream interpretations, telepathy, remote viewing, and communication through frequencies with ET visitors.

They were also training about reading stones. They learn to differentiate many types of stone on the mountain and in the valleys and those near the sea. They must learn to feel the difference and then the actual usage of each type of stone. They must communicate telepathically with the stone and find their vibration and their frequencies.

They would be brought to sacred places where Amaya could see hundreds and even thousands of huge stone each bigger than her hut house and they were all half buried firmly into the ground, standing tall and sturdy. There were sites where those stones were standing in circle and others snake shapes for ten miles and over and others seemed to be laying randomly on the open ground.

Amaya was told that all these huge stones were brought from very far away by the ancient extraterrestrial builders and each pattern were set up for a special reason. She was not told what was its purpose.

Life as a student in this esoteric school was exciting, busy, never a dull moment. In Amaya's group there were twelve students. The school comprised of many small buildings made mostly of wood and bamboo. Different buildings for different purpose. As for Amaya's group, the teachings were mostly outdoor. They would often go to the forest or where the stone circle stood and spend a lot of time learning and practicing using their mind and their own energy field.

After a full day of learning, discovery, practice, and more practice, Amaya would be so tired when she returned to her chamber that she would fall into deep sleep as soon as her head touch the pillow. Every morning she would jump up ready for more lessons. She absorbed knowledge like a thirsty sponge.

Once a year Amaya was allowed to go home to visit her family. She would choose the equinox celebration day so that she would meet all her cousins and childhood friends.

Four years soon passed, and it was graduation day for Amaya. She was sixteen years old. This was only graduation for the first level student. With this certificate she was qualified for a variety of jobs. She had the choice to be a teacher, to be an energy healer, or spiritual guide for adolescent.

She could choose to stay and live in town or go back and work in the village community.

There was an advance intensive training for another three years. This was only reserved for those who could pass more rigorous testing. After this course she would be awarded to title High Priest and that would mean a life of total dedication to spiritual work and spiritual teaching. Amaya would like that very much.

As attractive as that may be, deep inside of her she knew that this path was not for her right now because the role of a priestess required total celibacy and there was a nagging feeling that she needed to have a family of her own.

Internally, Amaya did have a big struggle because there was so much more she wanted to learn, but there was another little voice within her. "Get married and start a family," it said ever so softly.

She then remembered the year before when she went home, her mother reminded her that at age seventeen she was supposed to be married. That she was preparing her for this path. Also she and A'Hu had received many marriage proposals from nearby village and even as far as from town centre.

Amaya wondered what mating with a man would be like. Would she be scared? Would it be painful? Mother and daughter never discuss such matters, but she could see that mother and father were happy together. It was a good and long lasting union. Maybe she will find a man as good as her father. Who will that be?

Amaya stood naked and looked at herself in the mirror, something she rarely did. But now she wondered about her physical body. Would she be attractive to a man? What would they think of her? She wondered how do other people see her.

She was tall, with golden tan-coloured skin covered with a thin layer of oily sheen, which reflect light under the sun. She had medium-size firm breasts, black silken wavy long hair up to her small waist. Her face was oval shape, big brown eyes, high-arch black eyebrows, medium-size mouth, and pure ivory white well set teeth. From head to toe she was totally proportionate.

She thought, *Hmm, I think I do not look too bad.*

In fact, Amaya was the prettiest girl in the whole village. Not only that, her inner beauty was even better. She was kind and a great compassionate heart. Everyone wanted to be her friend.

After some more internal debate, she thought that she would wait until after graduation when she returned to her home village and have more discussions about the matter with her mother and then she will decide. She had time.

She would like to spend one year to put into practice what she had learned in school and then decide on a job and then marriage.

During one equinox spiritual gathering, Amaya was approached by a young man. It was a nice warm starry night. The bonfire was roaring away, sending sparks of amber light into all directions in the dark. Amaya was standing alone watching the stars. She could not recognize him at first, but when he started to talk to her, then she realized that he was one of her childhood friend. His name was A'Lua. He lived close by and so they used to meet and play with each other often until they had to leave home for school. He was two years older, so he left home first.

She had not seen him since he left, and suddenly he appeared in front of her, not a boy but a strong young man with muscular body and thick black wavy hair. He was very handsome, and Amaya was very much attracted to him.

Despite of the fact that he was trained as a captain in the military academy, his voice was gentle and smooth and Amaya was drowned into their conversation all through the night. There was so much to share—their mutual old days of fun and games, their separate lives in school, and so forth. Before they knew it, dawn had come and the singing started and that was the only time that they took their eyes off each other.

Well, after that night, there was no more internal debate. It was decided. She would marry A'Lua and that was that.

Marriage ceremony was simple and brief, but the celebration went on for three days and three nights. Family and friends from near and far all came to shower their well wishes on the newlyweds. There was no invitation sent out to anyone. The party was just opened to all who wished to come and many came.

It was on a green open lawn surrounded by rolling hills and tropical trees and flower bushes.

During the day, the guests would walk, talk, eat and play games all in a leisurely manner. During the night, they would start fire torches here and there and nice bonfire in the middle and they talk about the stars and High Spirits and sleep on the soft grass or on the self-provided hammocks among the trees.

Three days just flew by, and it was time to say goodbye to the mothers and fathers of the young couple, who would leave home and build their new "nest" somewhere else.

Amaya and A'Lua started their home in the city mainly because A'Lua's work at the military academy there and Amaya also got a teaching job in a city school.

The young happy couple enjoyed their new marriage life very much. After work there was time for meeting new friends, visiting cultural centres, libraries, and going to movies. When there were long holidays, they would travel to other cities or camp in the forest and climb the volcanic mountains.

One morning Amaya was dizzy and nauseous, and that feeling went on for days. She thought she was ill and was told later that she was pregnant. She was excited at the new experience, and her husband

A'Lua was overjoyed. Together they went back to their village to share this happy news with family and friends.

First pregnancy to Amaya was a nine-month biologic exploration and study. She noted down on paper every change in her body: the increasing stomach, the unnatural twisted curve of the spine causing back pain, the heavy womb causing sleepless night, the constant urination caused by pressed bladder, her breast grew like two big melons, her legs and ankle swollen, and, finally, the moving and gentle kicking of the little one as it grew bigger and bigger.

The time came for the birth. Mother came to help. Amaya felt pain. The kind of pain that was terrible at times and bearable at other times. The baby moved and kicked inside her body. The pain was becoming more and more intense and more and more often. At times she thought she could not breathe, and then as if everything, every bone and muscle from the waist down, was tearing apart. Water flowed, blood flowed. They could see the baby's head. They kept saying, "Push, push, push hard. Almost over now. One big push and it will be over."

Amaya used all her strength she never thought she had, and just when she thought she was going to faint, suddenly she heard a loud cry.

"It is a boy, and he is well."

With that announcement, Amaya felt relieved and went totally limp with exhaustion and yet she was elated and excited because she wanted to see the baby. All the pain and suffering was worth it.

When she held the baby in her arms, she felt such overwhelming love and joy that no word could describe.

"So this is motherhood. This is certainly something else. I salute all the women in the world especially my own mother."

And so that was the first baby, and over the years Amaya would have more children, seven in total. They were four boys and three girls. A'Lua loved children. As the family grew bigger, very often Maya would come and stay with them to help out. It was busy, but it was one big happy family.

Whenever possible Amaya and A'Lua would bring the family to nature. They would teach the children about the attribution of herbs and trees and how to navigate the forest. They sang songs to the trees and mountains.

They would camp there for days, soaking up the sunlight, swimming under the crystal-clear waterfalls, sleeping in the open field at night in the companionship of the stars and silver moon.

Time passed, and an ominous sign was in the air: rumours of corrupt government officials, stories of religious priests committing hideous crimes without being arrested because they were considered sacred and above the law, then religious and political factions split and fought among themselves.

Conflict and violence appeared on the news every day. There were control for territorial and domain clashes.

More often now A'Lua was called up for duty, and his presence in the family became less and less. Sometimes he would go off for a whole week and return totally exhausted and sometimes even injured. When this happened, Amaya and the children would give him the best of their tender loving care. Thus patched up, soon he was being called again and off he went.

Every time he left home Amaya worried that she may not see him return. Her heart ached, and often she cried alone silently at night. She missed him terribly.

At this point in time Amaya was the father and mother of the family attending to every physical and emotional need.

One day A'Lua came home hurriedly bringing horrible news of a big battle. He told Amaya and the children that they must prepare the family to leave any time. They must also warn their family and friends at the village. Not long after A'Lua's warning, they received news that many villages were burnt, farmland destroyed, and people killed during one or more battles.

Immediately Amaya brought her mother and father to live with her in the city, which was not totally safe also, but at least they were together. One day A'Lua was called up for service again. This time Amaya held him tight to her. She did not want to let him go. This time it was different from all those previous missions. They both looked at each other with teary eyes for a long time. One last embrace and he tore off. He never came back.

It was reported that he died in battle.

Amaya was devastated. She never thought that the pain of loss of a loved one could be so great and so deep. For days, weeks, and months she was in mourning. She was inconsolable. Her children missed their beloved father and cried often. Then she decided to bring the children and her parents to stay in the deep forest for a few months. *Let nature heal us*, she thought.

When they returned she found that life in the city became unbearable. Due to constant fighting, transport was disrupted, causing food and water shortage.

Then Amaya decided that they needed to move to a safer place where they could grow their own food and children could be homeschooled by her.

They found a quiet village rather far away from the city, and there they lived in peace for the next ten of years.

Meanwhile, her mother passed away due to old age, followed soon by the passing of her father too.

By this time her children grown and all got married. They each built their own houses, some with their own farmland and domestic animals. All the children and grandchildren lived in the same village.

Amaya lived alone nearby so that it would be easy for her grandchildren to visit and spend time with her. She loved to tell them stories of nature and High Spirits. She taught them to sing to the sun and the moon and the stars just like the way her mother taught her when she was small.

News of a big war, the final battle, the Armageddon, was about to occur. Amaya was worried and had long discussions with her children about precautions and defence, but everything that they could do was in fact quite useless.

Fear spread like wild fire everywhere. Then one day the ET angels came and said to Amaya, "You must all leave or you will die. We are conducting a mass evacuation for those who are willing to go. We will fly."

They were then taken along with many hundreds of families on a very big spaceship and transported to a new land far away.

When they all arrived the angels said, "Here is a fertile land. Here you will live in peace, and there will be no shortage of food and water. You will start a new community and build a new life for yourself. We will come often and give you all the necessary materials and knowledge that you may need." Then they left.

Years came and gone. Houses were built; and healing centre, schools and temple for spiritual practice were set up. There was indeed plenty of natural food, and ET often introduced new seeds to add on the variety. They also brought in the animals, the goats, and even cattle later on.

The community lived in peace, and Amaya continued her herbal and energy healing practice. There was no government or organized religion. Everyone lived according to the nature way—the gentle way.

One day Amaya went up to the mountain alone and looking down at the valley village where they lived she felt a sense of fulfilment. She felt accomplished. She had a very rich life, one that consisted of joy, grief, pain, loss, love, expectation, disappointment, and so forth.

This is a good time to leave, she thought.

She lay down on a patch of soft grass, looked at the blue sky, and went into a very deep sleep. The soul emerged from her ninety-year-old female body and became Sprkle again.

He went back to his home base and called up Purple Flame. "Well, looking at the past journey, what have you learned?" "Much," said the student.

"Pray tell."

"I found the biological changes of a female was most interesting and amazing to experience. From a girl child, to young adult, to womanhood, to experience sexual intercourse with a male body, then pregnancy, then the actual birth itself was most exhilarating. I never thought there could be such a lot of changes in one body."

"And the babies? How come you wanted so many children?"

"I don't know. Perhaps the banana tree syndrome was still in my memory."

"Ha, ha, ha."

"What of the emotional aspect of a woman?"

"Well, I cried a lot. Not only when I was sad, and also when I was happy. I think the emotional sensitivity of a woman is much higher than a man, not to mention the intuition level is much higher than any living species on Earth.

"In this journey there was so much emotional experiences like deep joy, deep grief, elation, fear, pain of the broken heart, worries, and so forth. It was overall a very precious life experience. Thank you, my teacher, for making it possible. I feel I had filled a big chapter in my book after this life."

"Now that you are back up here, would you not like to see what had happened to the land of Mua?"

"Oh yes, indeed."

From the Akashic Record, Sprkle could see the whole picture of Mua and the cataclysmic events that befell her.

The war between the political and religious factions became one of uncontrollable ferocity. It was like destruction of the most maddening kind.

There were the unceasing explosions. Afterwards, cities and towns became rubbles of dead stones, farmland scorched, forest burnt, and then came the earthquakes, the breaking up of the land mass. Then at the very end, the ocean, like an enormous monster, opened its huge wide mouth and swallowed the whole continent utterly and totally and sent her down, down into her dark bowel of the abyss.

Millions died on land and in the sea. Mua was no more.

Atlan

Sprkle turned his attention to the second new continent on the other side of the planet. Although this land appeared almost the same time as Mua, it was not seeded with life until three thousand years later.

It seemed like it was Mua's younger brother. Its name was Atlan. Even though it was seeded with life later, it evolved very quickly and very soon was able to catch up with the rest of the world as a fine specimen of a new civilization. Atlan was in the west part of the globe, and Mua situated on the east.

The landscape of Atlan was picture perfect. There was lush green land, plants of all kinds, rivers and a long coastline facing an ocean. There were land animals and sea creatures. One can see the natural life of Atlan was that of abundance.

Everything about Atlan was new. The dominant human population was the descendant of the subhuman race of Alanian. Hence, they were Star Seed Human born with very high mind power.

Sprkle also observed that the people living on the northern part of the continent had fair even milky white skin and light-coloured hair, even blonde, and their eyes were big and coloured also. Some had green eyes and some had blue.

For those living on the south, which was warmer and tropical climate, people there had brown skin, honey coloured hair and big brown eyes.

The Galactic Council kept a close eye on this new creation. They were careful in the seeding program this time around. Apart from the new Atlan human, they also allowed advance star travellers and star visitors to dwell on this land so as to maintain a balance of spiritual awareness and practical science.

For about ten thousand years, this arrangement worked well and Atlan thrived and the people prospered.

Sprkle moved time forward and found that the balance of culture had changed. Those of the scientific camp had grown very powerful, and they were making experiments on the human genome. The result was that millions of new hybrids that were animals/human, plant/human, and other indescribable monsters roamed the land.

This condition had caused much concerned to the Angelic Guardian. They had to deal with the souls of these monsters that were not human and not animals. After death they would be needed to be recalibrated mostly to the lower dimensions back to animals and plants. This was not foreseen when they introduced the advance genetic technology to the Atlanean.

Sprkle here moved time to one important day.

This day the sky over Earth was bright-red colour. The normal golden sunlight was totally obscured. Then to the horror of the seashore dwellers, when they looked up to the sky, they saw a massive ball of raging fire falling down toward them at great speed. Soon every one living in north, south, east, and west of the land saw it.

Everybody ran to all different directions. Some jumped into the sea water, some tried to hide in caves or under big trees. Anywhere and everywhere human and creatures were trying their best to hide from this ball of hell fire.

As the fireball approached closer, everything started to heat up. The intensity of the heat was so powerful that soon all animals that flew in the air started to fall en masse, like raining dead birds everywhere. Next, trees started to burn. Then when the trees were gone, the land animals, human, everything that was out in the open were totally singed or turned to charcoal.

Next, a colossal asteroid hit the ground and the whole planet shook from pole to pole. A succession of earthquakes everywhere on the whole continent.

The point of impact was the southwest of the big continent. The asteroid sank into the sea, bringing with it a huge piece of the continent and its inhabitants to a deep water grave.

Sprkle moved his attention to the day after all the calamity was over. He saw that the big continent was still there. There was an enormous hole on the southwest of the land like a big volcanic ring filled with water. To the north, east, and west, the landscape became barren. After the earthquakes and volcanic activities, there were more mountains. The whole land mass was smaller than before. The sea had risen considerably over the years.

Most sea creatures were dead or fried. The monster hybrids were all gone. Those human who survived came back to the surface from the underground world, and they moved to other lands to the east and some moved to the west.

Here Sprkle jumped time forward when Atlan was again being seeded with life. The Angelic Council was working on the next phase of the Atlan experiment. This time the new human race was only given barren land, rivers, and basic plants for survival. No more advance technology, at least for the beginning.

Human must learn through working and living in harmony with nature and appreciate what they have by creating themselves. This time they were not given a paradise on a silver platter.

For seeding the land, this time they brought in the descendants of the Mua people, who were more spiritually inclined and great energy healers. Following that they brought in also star beings from the higher dimensions, the fifth and sixth and also people from the older and more stable civilization of other star systems even from other galaxies.

There will also be science, but they would keep a tighter control on the progress.

For the next five thousand years, peace and growth prevailed on Atlan. The Northern Muan, who were pale skinned, blend in well with the blonde Atlanean.

They interbred well, and many generations of highly evolved people came. After hundreds of years, the descendants of the Muan and Atlanean were able to build a great civilization on the land. Atlan rose again.

The energy that was used to run the cities were not enough. Atlan had grown so much and the population so wide spread that they needed more fuel.

In view of this dilemma, the Guardian began to teach the scientific team to tap into a source of good clean and sustainable energy from crystals. Atlan had a vast deposit of crystals right under its feet. All they had to do was to learn how to mine them and also how to extract power from the massive blocks.

And so the Crystal Culture of Atlan began. This new source of energy enabled Atlan's civilization to progress in great leaps.

And then the Atlanean learned to use the crystal to develop laser weapons that could destroy objects in an instant.

Years passed, and more and more experiments were conducted on the laser light until one day came powerful guns that could shoot thousands of miles away. They could destroy the whole city in one shot. Greed of power overcame the warriors and the scientists.

During this period in time the Atlan civilization was progressing to its peak point. There were beautiful cities with amazing architecture of all kinds imaginable. There were schools that offered teachings to satisfy all kinds of interest and curiosity—new ideas, new creations, new experiments, new products, and so forth. Creative talent was held very high in society and allowed to run totally unbridled.

There was one huge central temple that was used for energy work. Here, special priestesses and priests would work on night and day shifts to maintain the crystalline vibration to a safe balance for everyone.

Life was generally good. There was no lack of food. Most people lived in the cities, and they were free to construct their own house and choose the kind of work that was suitable to them. Each city hub was built in such a way that people did not need to travel too far to work and socialize with friends and families.

There was thriving art culture. New visual art technique was introduced and new products came on stream every day. Musical instruments were tested, and new sounds and rhythm were tried and played. Art galleries and musical halls were everywhere.

For more spiritually inclined there were at least one temple in every hub where one can learn about the Law of the Universe, about reincarnation of souls, the reality of dreams, and other dimensional worlds and so forth.

The seaports were always busy with trading ships of all sizes from foreign lands far and near. Foreign goods were brought to the population. Shops were filled with precious stones, fine jewelleries of gold and silver, refine cloths like silk and cotton for high fashion, these and many other products to satisfy the most exquisite taste.

At this time life on Atlan was prosperous, peaceful and generally good. On the other hand, unbeknown to most population, the elite government officials and the belligerent military faction were becoming restless. The black head of power and greed was rising, and there was planning and plotting of an invasion of another land. Atlan needed to expand, and if they were going to take on another nation, why not the biggest? Why not Mua?

By this time Mua was an older civilization with a population that were literate and well trained and with a level of civil prosperity equal to none, not to mention the huge land mass with great potential. One thing that Atlanian wanted very much was a type of sound technology that they did not have. They must have them.

They set a date to beam a massive and powerful laser to destroy part of a city as a show of force and then move in with the troops.

The fateful date came. All the procedures were set, and the red button ready to go off. Someone pressed it, and the beam shot out and hit an unknown target, probably Mua. No one knew at this point. What happened next was not supposed to happen.

There was a reflection of the laser light. There was a mirror or another crystal on the other end. The beam shot back with full force, and a massive explosions hit home base. Atlan went to pieces. The ocean water rushed in to claim it.

All her beauty, her splendour, her power, and pride sank.

In the aftermath, three higher peaks of the land protruded on the sea surface and these were the remainder islands.

This was the third stage of the story of Atlan. The years that followed for those survivors on the islands were that of hunger and misery.

Many of the Atlanean built boats and migrated to other lands, and they began to rebuild their lives there. Hundreds of years passed, and their descendants later on returned to the three islands. The dark angelic warriors wanted to reclaim the lost technologies of the crystals.

After years of research and experiments, they acquired the knowledge of drawing power from the Earth's core crystal. With this power they will invade and conquer other countries in the hope of rebuilding Atlan to its former glory.

However, this was not to be. These new and young generations of Atlanean were not able to harness and control the mighty power of Earth's core crystal.

During one all important experiment, someone made a small mistake in the process. One fraction of the calculation was wrong. One switch was flicked too soon, and suddenly explosion flared followed by successive fires, and the whole energy grid of the land cracked open. Mother Earth quaked in response. Tsunami followed and swallowed the last three islands and all her people.

Atlan became none.

From then on Atlan was just a story, a legend. There were bits and pieces of information that surfaced occasionally from people's faded memory, but everything about it was misty, shady.

"Did it actually exist?" people ask nowadays.

As for the Earth, her planetary generator at the very centre was interfered causing another planetary tilt, which led to wild and extreme earthquakes, volcanic eruption and fire, followed by ice, followed by global floods.

Once again Earth stood still.

Seeing this, Sprkle felt sad and a sense of loss. He asked Purple Flame, "Why this is so?"

His teacher replied, "It is human nature to reach always higher. Toward the highest peak he strives. What comes after the peak?"

"The fall," said Sprkle.

FROM ASHES SHE ROSE AGAIN

Sprkle continued to observe Earth on a global scale. In order for him to learn the full story of Earth, at least the main events, it was only possible that he study through the Records in the Hall of Universal Memory. It was not possible on ground level. From the holographic image, he saw the fantastic plan the Celestial Beings of Love had for this fragile blue planet.

He was deeply touched by the dedication and perseverance the collective Celestial Elders, the Galactic Council, the Angelic Healers, and the host of other angels shown in assisting Earth toward her upward path.

Time and time again this small, fragile blue planet, was blown off, knocked down, tilted at her axis (twice), her orbit erratic like no other, burnt to the ground, or frozen stiff; and each time the collective Beings of Love came to help her mend her broken body. And with her own power and determination, Mother Terra rose up again and again to rebuild herself whole and beautiful.

Sprkle said, "Mother Earth is indeed the biggest hero of all time. She is my hero. This is great lesson for me—unconditional love and perseverance."

The Nation of the Nile (Around 53,000 BCE)

While Atlan and Mua were in their heyday, the Celestial Elders and the Galactic Council planned to build a series of monumental structures to form a new and more powerful energy grids across the planet Earth.

This grand project was to assist the planet and her children to boost their vibrational frequency in their energy field in alignment with the Ascension program.

They scanned everywhere and found a specific area that was actually the centre point of the whole planet. They decided that it was there that they will build the new portal and a new crystal power generator. It would be the biggest and most powerful sphere of vibrational frequency. The energy field in this sphere is not only used to stabilize the planet, it will also be used as a bridge of light that align to Sirius B star system. This alignment, together with the interstellar star gates, would facilitate the Guardians and Warriors of Light to leap through time making travel to Earth instantaneous. Through this teleportation centre, star cruisers could travel to any planets, stars, and galaxies in the universe. No other planet in the solar system has it. Earth was the only chosen one.

To house and protect these all important creation, the Galactic Council invited the assistance from the star families who were specialized in buildings and architectures.

They arrived and brought along special aircrafts and their tools of the trade. They wanted to use the hardest and the best stone so that the structure will last forever. They would use the finest granite for the structure and cover the whole surface with the best white marble.

They found the best quarry for the chosen stones. They used laser and saser beam waves to cut each piece of stone to precise measurement according to their plan. Then they used antigravity technology to transport to the desired site.

Very soon a super structure in pyramid form was constructed. It was sitting on the geographical centre of the planet Earth itself. It was covered with the most exquisite white marble with a pure gold capstone. On a sunny day this grand pyramid was covered with the most glorious white and golden light that can be seen for miles away.

Next two smaller pyramids were created on the sides in order to make the star alignment to Sirius. Thereafter, some more smaller pyramids were also built around that area. When the pyramids were finished, the Angelic Council went to work on the Bridge and the star gates. Huge crystals were brought in also. One was put inside the centre of the pyramid, then four outside in the Nile River water that served as electro conductor. When everything was set in place and charged up. The light beam that shot through the golden capstone of the Big Pyramid went up so high in the sky that it could be seen beyond the local star systems.

The pyramid system works both ways. Energy can be transmitted as well as channelled from space through the crystal to energise the ground and beyond. It is a transmitter and a receiver.

Thus satisfied, the Galactic Council decided that they will build a nation on this land. This will be a nation like no other in the history of the world. Atlan would be like a dwarf in comparison. They will call this nation Egypt.

When the Angelic Watchers first came, this place was already lush green with very fertile soil. Wild plants and fruits were abundant. There were animals big and small of all kinds. There were small communities of earthling human, mainly hunters and gatherers living in primitive thatched huts. They were nomads. When the river grew big and swamp the banks, they would leave and returned when the Nile ebbed.

So this was the condition at the time, and the angels said, "We are going to change all this."

One day on a remote island far away, a man had a dream. He dreamt that an angel of light came to him and told him to bring his family and his extended families to go east. They would walk or sail or take whatever means they could. There was a paradise waiting for them. They did not need to stay on this semi-barren island suffering harsh weather condition and a poor existence. They should go straight east, follow the Star Sirius, and they will see from a distance a great pyramid structure and they will make a new wonderful life there. The soil is rich and easy to till, wild plants and fruits plentiful. Fish of all kinds are easy reach. No one would be hungry there.

The man woke up and packed the little that he had and brought his family and friends to go on a journey to a happy new life.

Little did he know that there were hundreds like him. They were all making the big journey to the new land of milk and honey. He also did not know that the reason he and others were called was because they were all the descendants of the people of Mua and Atlan. Thus, a big migration began.

Sprkle asked his teacher Purple Flame, "Why were these people chosen and not others?"

He explained, "These two human races carried the original genetic imprint of the first Astral Human in Tara. This genetic lineage could not be allowed to stop due to the continuation of the Ascension program. Despite of the ever-changing cycles of war and peace, destruction and rebuilding of the planet Earth, the unceasing cycles of death and reseeding of life, after thousands upon thousands of experiments, through millions of trials and errors, still the Galactic Council would not give up. The Law of Ascension must be upheld. Do you understand, Sprkle?"

"Yes, my good teacher, I remember and am learning much. I will now observe further. Thank you."

Purple Flame disappeared.

The first batch of new immigrants first came to the delta area where the Nile meet the Mediterranean Sea, and soon hundreds became thousands, and the communities were moving up along the riverbank.

All the time the Angelic Guardians were monitoring the progress. They provided what was needed at the time. Apart from basic needs of better seeds for planting food, animals and cattle, they saw that people needed education.

They introduced language. They were taught to carve little figures, like birds, plants, everything that they could see in their surroundings. Next, they gave them sound. One sound, one word for one picture. After language came schools.

Then schools and temples were built.

They needed good governance, rules and regulations, and so more buildings were erected where the scribes and law keepers would work and live in.

Then there were huge buildings dedicated for science and technologies. Somehow most of the Atlan descendants excelled in this field. Teachers were sent in from other star system.

For the spiritually inclined people, spectacular temples were built. The Urtite wise men were invited to teach the way of the spiritual path.

At this point Sprkle called up Purple Flame who appeared instantly. "Teacher, I would like to ask permission to incarnate as a full male adult so that I could again join the priests from Ur to teach the people. I would like to experience life as an Egyptian. I also want to contribute to raising the spiritual growth of the new nation."

"Yes, this is a good time to go. I will make the necessary arrangement."

The high Urtite priest was informed of the appearance of Sprkle and his participation in the work of the brotherhood. There was no introduction needed as they knew him from way back when.

Sprkle arrived, and he was at awe when he saw the magnificent temple. It was immense to start with and then the spectacular carvings and frescos on the walls and pillars. He had never experienced such grandeur in all his past lives.

He thought, *Life here will be very interesting. So much beauty and so much to learn.*

His daily routine would be to wake up before sun rise, had a communal meal of barley bread and vegetable, afterwards prayer in the special hall with pillars and a dome that opened to the sky. In the afternoon would be teaching until evening. After evening meal would be individual meditation. Sometimes he would go to the hillside to observe the stars. Bedtime was flexible, so he chose to sleep late.

It was a uniform routine life. Food and clothing were simple, but it was all he needed. After some years he realized how much he enjoyed teaching. Every day he would prepare the subjects with great enthusiasm and anxiously looked forward to the next class.

He had made a list of the subjects that he would like to teach, and they would be

What is Spirit and what is Soul,

Self Empowerment,

The Law of One,

Reincarnation,

Life after Death,

The Real Home for the Souls,

and so forth.

On the first day he was brought to an amphitheatre in an open area surrounded by flowers and fauna and palm trees. Students were sitting and talking in semicircle.

He would stand in the middle of the stage. The sunlight was warm and bright. It was just perfect.

When Sprkle started he had about twenty students. Soon the number multiplied, and his class was so popular that after three months, there was standing room only in the amphitheatre.

Sprkle's life experience as an Egyptian was a fulfilling journey. His soul left the body at age sixty. He returned as a ball of light to his home base on the fourth dimension so that it would be easier for him to reincarnate the next time.

In a matter of a few hundred years, Egypt grew from a small hunter community into villages and then big towns, then cities each with its schools, marvellous temples, fantastic palaces, colourful art galleries, majestic buildings beaming with illumination like jewels among beautiful lush gardens all along the River Nile, and so forth.

With the big multidimensional portals in place, those who died and needed recalibration of the souls in the Healing Zone of Sirius B were able to be channelled through them. Thereon these souls would return to the fifth dimension and did not need to reincarnate if so choosing. These souls were free. No more seals and chains on their Personal Energy Field. Without the Bridge Zone Portal, this could not be possible.

Then it came to be the age of the constellation Leo. In honour of the Leonide celestial entities, a special structure in the shape of an enormous lion was constructed. It was a body and huge head with long mane of a lion. It was awesome to behold. It was also built in total alignment to the Sirius B star system.

Inside this super lion they built the biggest library in the world. This was not ordinary library. The knowledge was vast and most advance in the universe. This was encoded in a certain sound frequency. Only those in the know or the chosen few that were given the Key could have the access.

The interstellar star gates remained open. The star visitors were flying in and out with their super spaceships. They did everything they could to assist what was needed on the ground to grow in peace and stability.

With the guidance and loving care of the Angelic Council, Egypt flourished economically, culturally, and spiritually. At this point in time there was no other civilization on the planet that could match it.

This was indeed the Era of Divine Egypt. Ten thousand years came and gone quickly.

Sprkle turned his attention to the holographic sphere and focused on a time of special occurrence.

He saw images of spaceships, big and small, from the Orion star system. They looked menacing and aggressive. They were hovering in the sky above Egypt.

The Nibiruan and their royal entourage had returned to Earth. They needed more gold for their planet. They landed where gold was near and that was Upper Egypt. As soon as they landed, they restarted their tyrannical ways just as before. They established a new god religion cult in Egypt. With their ability to fly, their superhuman power, and their ability to exude brilliant light around their bodies, they stroke fear to the local native people. They demanded worship and sacrificial offerings of blood and gold. They created a priesthood called the Brotherhood of Serpent. They raised temples and pyramids to serve their purposes.

And then the Nephilin also came. They came to take the star gates. These important "Doors" that facilitate instant time travel had always been a target of possession for the Dark Force, their POWR Federation. Now they came with one goal in mind—to take the Great Pyramid and its super star gate.

Soon battles broke out between upper and lower Egypt. Then they attacked the Great Pyramid to gain access of the star gates.

The Warriors of Light came.

Weapons of mass destruction were used on both sides.

At the end, the Great Pyramid was damaged but the Warriors of Light maintained control of the star gates. However, the alignment to Sirius B was off.

Once again the Galactic Warriors won the day, and the Nibiruan was banned to a planet far away. The Nephilin and their Dark Force dispersed and retreated to their home base, the Shadow. But before they surrendered many escaped to colonize other lands. They brought along with them some of the military faction.

Sprkle moved time forward to 5,500 BC.

New great pyramids and new portals were erected to align with Alcyon, the Pleiadian star system, to free trapped and damaged souls. The original Sphinx that was damaged by war and flood was reconstructed on the same site.

This time the new portal was guarded by a special race of angelic human beings called the Celestial Melchisedeck.

Forward to 3,000 BC, and Egypt became the land of plenty and high culture again. Peace prevailed for about a thousand years. By this time no longer god as kings, the dynastic pharaohs of men began. The first few dynasties had good kings. They were primarily builders and maintained a policy of protection and provision for the populace.

But centuries of wealth and power brought decadence and laziness to the royal descendants along with their religious priests. They became corrupt and degenerate.

Temples built originally for spiritual knowledge turned into superstitious worships, blood sacrifices, and trading posts. The religious ceremonies for life after death were invented to instill fear. Technique that guaranteed a place in heaven were bought and sold through the temples everywhere.

Religious priests, especially the Brotherhood of the Serpent, were fat and rich.

The Galactic Guardians were seeing that all their effort to raise the vibration of the populace was failing. They could not allow this to continue, because the down spiral of the vibration of souls would affect the vibrational pattern of the Earth itself.

Sprkle again called for Purple Flame to explain, and he said, "You remember the Ascension Program, which is part of the Law of Universe, that I had explained before? Well, there is a fix pattern how everything works in the cosmos.

"During this time, it is essential that the vibration of planet Earth and her children be raised to a higher level in order for her Ascension Program to continue. Therefore, for those who wishes to ascend going down in vibration was not an option. There was a strict universal timeline that they had to meet, and this is why the pyramids of Egypt are so important. The big crystals brought there are used to feed high frequency energy to the planet as well as the population.

"The Ascension Program is that every 26,556 years there is a total alignment of all the multidimensional portals and that is the time when they would be all open. That would be the golden opportunity for everyone and everything from the tiniest of planet to galaxies to pass through the multidimensional portals to a higher dimension. Those in the fourth dimension will move up to the fifth and those in the fifth move to the sixth and so forth. However, one must raise their vibrational frequency to meet the higher portal's requirement. To be able to pass through the fifth portal to go to the fifth dimension, one's frequency must be equal to that. "Right now Earth's frequency is not high enough. Therefore, much has to be done yet, not only in Egypt but over on the eastern part of the globe there are also problems.

"So you see, Sprkle, there is much at stake here. It is also why there had been so many wars and attacks everywhere by the Dark Force for control of star gates and dimensional portals they want to shut them down or destroy them to prevent planets and stars that are in their dominion to move up and out of their control. You see? They cannot move up anywhere. They can only move down and down. In any case, this was their choice."

"What happen if Earth miss this time line?"

"She must wait for another 26,556 years. You must know that she missed the last cycle due to war and destruction. Her vibrational frequency was too weak, and it was not possible to meet the frequency required to pass through the portal. This time is different. She must complete her mission."

"That would be disastrous. How can I help?"

"You will help if you are willing. We will discuss further. In any case, even as we speak, the Angelic Council is at work to turn the situation around. Look on and you will see that an avatar from the ninth dimension was chosen to be born on Earth as a king as well as the highest spiritual leader in Egypt. His name is Ahken, born 1,398 BC. His first and foremost mission was to reintroduce the Law of One and all the original spiritual teachings by ending the corrupt practice of those false prophets at the temples. His emblem would be a round golden disc emitting rays of life in all directions. This was to represent the One Source of Life.

"The other mission would be to work with the SERRES to introduce a special set of spiritual rites so as to raise the vibration of the population, at least as many as possible. This teaching and practice was supposed to be free for all indiscriminately."

Sprkle continued looking at the holographic scanner with hope and anticipation that all will be well.

In the beginning everything was working smoothly. All those who were able to practice the Ascension Rites were able to dispel their dark contaminated energy in their energy field and raise their soul frequencies at the Healing Zone. Their souls after physical death would be able to ascend and return to their original dimension through the Bridge Portal.

Meanwhile, the old cult established by the Brotherhood of the Serpent felt threatened by Ahken's new religious power. They tried every way to block his every move. They undermined his plan and projects at every turn. Then Ahken had no choice but to build a new temple in another land far from them.

With the new temple and home base established, Ahken was able to work freely and accomplished his mission admirably. In the beginning, people came in hundreds and then thousands. They all wanted salvation. What was more attractive was that the rites and technique were free of charge. For the first time people were hopeful. They were confident that after death they will be free and return to heaven. The door of heaven will be opened to all, even the poorest of the poor.

In view of the growing power of Ahken and the serious drainage of gold coins in their coffers, the corrupt priests sent spies and infiltrated his court. They fanned family jealousy and feud among his wife and concubines. Soon they were in open conflict among them, and Ahken was murdered along the way.

After his death the Egyptian ascension program was in chaos. The teaching of salvation was thrown out to the desert sands, and the Brotherhood of the Serpent revived their previous dark practice. And so it was for many years.

Egypt went on a downward spiral. Save from the angelic humans who continued to guard the temples that house the portals and pyramids, the rest of the nation was spinning down to corruption, slavery, debaucheries, drug addiction, material greed, murders. All kinds of crimes were committed by the royals, the rich, as well as the poor.

Wars between Egypt and the neighbouring countries went on continuously for centuries. Apart from one or two that were powerful and managed a long reign through ruthlessness and cruelty, the rest of the dynasties changed so often that the pharaohs barely had time to warm their throne.

Even the Egyptian dynastic records were changed many times. Those that were not favourable to the current government were wiped out from the history books of stone.

Then one final war broke out. The war of the gods. The Fallen Ones against the Galactic Warriors. Once again a ferocious fight for control of the super star gate inside the Great Pyramid. The end result was all the pyramids were destroyed and the important portals were captured. The POWR Federation from the higher dimension spread a Dark Energy net all around Earth. She is being captured and colonized, nothing goes in or out without the Federation permission.

From this time forward, high vibrational energy waves from the Angelic Council would not be able to penetrate the dark energy net to reach even the surface of the planet and the world population was put in spiritual slumber. Amnesia and total mind control from cradle to grave. What is worse is the incessant reincarnation into the 3D world reality.

With the powerful tight grip of the new energy grid in place, the planet will see the rise of another round of Dark Age.

In later years the Nephilin and other members of the POWR Federation rebuilt the pyramids, aligning them to their home base, the Orion system. The Sphinx was re-build with the face of the current pharaohs.

And then nature intervened. The natural cycle of Earth's climate change arrived. There were years of draughts followed by years of floods. Extreme hot and cold weather persisted for decades. At the end, Egypt lay in ruins. The once magnificent pyramids and palaces were nothing but heaps of stone. They became empty structures, a faded memory of a once glorious past.

In the meantime, in the higher Celestial Realm, hot discussion was taking place. The big question was, "What is it going to be? Time is of the essence, save Earth and her children? Save just the planet and let the degenerates take the natural course to hell, or continue to revive, repair and reseed?"

The debate carried on for a long time without any unanimous agreement.

Seeing no firm decision anywhere, Sprkle turned his attention to something else that was more interesting.

The Civilization of Maya

"What is the Maya?" Sprkle wondered and moved the time line back a bit and watched.

The ancient advance culture of Maya was part of the grand project of the Galactic Council to build a continuous Energy Lei Line on the planet to raise its vibrational frequency.

The Great Pyramid of Egypt was the first power base being in the geographical centre of the planet. From this point, stretching to north, south, east, and west overseas and land, many pyramids and mystical crystal circles were built and natural structures like mountains and lakes were created as part of the line.

As for the stone structures, the Angelic Builders, armed with the successful plan that built the Great Pyramid and other great temples, used the same method and same type of stones to build the immense pyramids all over the globe along the planetary Lei Line. Everything was connected, forming a continuous powerful energy grid all around the planet.

This project was collectively called the Civilization of the Maya. The high priests; the Wise One; the Star Gazers; and advance scientists from Atlan, Mua, and Egypt during their golden age period were encouraged to participate and to migrate to all those lands where the power structures were.

Dimensional portals were built in secret spaces underneath many of the pyramids, temples, mountains, and lakes. The chosen people would be the guardian of the Lei Line and the portals where ever they were assigned to go.

Soon a great migration around the globe took place. These people were told to populate and build new nations. They would be provided with everything needed. The star benevolent beings would be their constant companion.

And so many great nations and wonderful culture mushroomed from the centre point of Egypt. The new culture and civilizations expanded to the far east and to the far west covering even the polar regions.

This was the true Golden Era, the grand Mayan civilization. Thousands of years gone by quickly.

On the negative side, Sprkle observed:

After the fall of Atlan and Egypt, the aggressive warriors, mostly made up of members of the former Atlan military and Egyptian corrupt priests, the Brotherhood of Serpent, migrated to the Andes Mountain valleys, conquered all the lands there, and then moved south of the continent along the mountain range in the south and captured the magnificent pyramids and temples that the Angelic Builders set up during the Mayan civilization era.

Once established the warriors started their rule of terror. They waged war and conquered peaceful and religious cities and towns. They plundered, promoted mass killing, slavery, and human sacrifices. This was the Aztec and the Incas era. The true Mayan people left even before they arrived.

The following thousands of years of many wars on Earth, the previous teachings for higher evolution and self-empowerment was suppressed by evil and tyrannical rulers. The same was happening worldwide.

Many big nations became many small tribes and kingdoms, each with their own respective chief or small king. They created their own beliefs and gods and demanded worship and offerings. Each small kingdom will possess their own warriors and with that they would battle each other for more slaves, food, and land.

Conflicts and battles were unceasing for centuries. Farmers and peasants were plucked out to fight, and as a result food production was low. Millions of civilians died of starvation or died in the battlefields. This dire condition was everywhere. Nations of the East, Middle East, West, and far West of the planet were all seem to be falling into the abyss of decline.

This was the era of many kingdoms and many kings. This was a very grim period indeed.

The Wheel of Time passed.

The Bringers of Love/ Light
(1,500 BCE and Forward to about 9 BCE)

Sprkle was getting very anxious at this point. He was worried that if nothing was done soon Earth may just as well miss her Ascension Time Line again. He called Purple Flame, and he came to calm him.

"There is a plan in place. The Celestial Elders in the Rishi realm (beyond the thirteen dimension) have decided to do something. In view of the dark energy grid around the planet, high frequency cannot come from above, an alternative way to bring Light and raise vibration of the populace is to work on the ground level. Angelic beings can go through the 4d frequency incarnate as human and affect the energy from within the planet and its people. This is a slow process, but this is a start."

"The Melchizedeck, a collective of titanic Light Brilliance of the thirteenth dimension, will intervene. They will create a highly spiritual group called the Brotherhood of Light who will then create a new race of beings, mainly Star Seeds, the Children of Light. These souls will not be affected by the grid. They will be born fully awake and aware of their spiritual mission.

"The Brotherhood of Light also created spiritual schools in the Himalayan mountain valleys, north India, and the Tibetan mountain communities. Wise Souls from the higher dimensions were incarnated and were brought in to these areas to help the teaching work. They spoke the words of wisdom, of love and compassion.

"In India there was the revival of the ancient sacred knowledge of the Rig-Veda. From this many branches of Yoga developed over thousands of years by many students/teachers/yogis.

"The teaching mainly involved eight principal practices:

1. Morality
2. Self-Discipline - contentment, purity of the heart and mind
3. Asceticism and learning
4. Posture
5. Breath control
6. Sense withdrawal
7. Concentration
8. Meditation
9. Joy and bliss

"Then a special avatar from the ninth dimension incarnated to teach about self-awareness, the way to transcend the mundane mind to the higher divine mind, the way to connect with the Divine Light within the self, to expand one's vision to see the universe through meditation.

They called the teacher Buddha, and thus Buddhism was born. Millions of followers and thousands of schools and temples were established in honour of this great teacher, even after the teacher's soul left his body.

"As time passed, this wonderful teaching spread all over the kingdoms in and around the Himalaya valleys. And later on, through the opening of the Silk Road, it was introduced to the Far Eastern kingdoms, but in this area the teaching did not take root.

However, in about 500 BCE, the continent of the Far East, another avatar teacher appeared. He was Lao Ze. Born of the land since young, he understood the way of the local people.

"It was difficult time of warring tribal warlords, fiefdoms, battles, widespread slavery, and so forth. Poverty and starvation was everywhere. The people were downtrodden, abused, desperate, hopeless, and lifeless. It was in this grim condition that he came.

"Lao Ze was a lone traveller. He gave dispensations and messages of compassion, tolerance, technique of raising self-awareness, self empowerment, social justice, the way to live in peace and brought hope to strengthen the people's heart.

"He knew astrology and he could prophesy the future. He was constantly sought after by kings and warlords for his wisdom. He served under one king in the Shou emperor's court, but he was disappointed when he saw that he only wanted power. He left and thereafter avoided all governments and royal calling.

"The most notable teaching of Lao Ze was the Way (Dao De Jing):
The Way to achieve contentment that leads to true happiness
The Way of the path to Ascension The Path to the Light
The Path back to the One

Through Lao Ze many schools were set up in later years to teach the wisdom of the Way. He was succeeded by Kung Fu Zi (Confucius), who continued his great works.

"And then there was the Book of Change (I Ching), which was treasured and continuously studied loyally by the scholars in the old as well modern time.

"Over to the Western continent, the new astronomers and astrologers sprang up. Schools of the Mayan culture, ancient messages from the stars carved in stones.

"In the area of the Mediterranean, he saw peace and widespread trading by rich traders. The most well-known were the Phoenicians. Through their maritime trading route, they connected and opened multicultural exchanges among many different nations.

"In Greece he saw great teachers of philosophy, modern science, languages, and so forth. The most well-known were, Plato, Pythagoras, Socrates, and many others. There were many great buildings dedicated for new learnings. There were huge libraries housing thousands and thousands of scrolls and steles ready to lift the minds and hearts of the seekers.

"Then spread across the globe, there were the spiritual healers, the Shamans, the Druids, the desert Aborigine, and so forth—all contributed to the transcendence of the mind of humanity."

Sprkle was happy to see all these bursting of spiritual life like a blanket of wonderful light over humanity.

He called this the Era of Enlightenment.

The good life did not last for long, however. Two hundred years down the line, a young warrior decided to rule the world. His army brought about a blanket of terror and bloodshed from Macedonia all the way to India. He was the first of the European empire builder and soon others will follow.

Then Purple Flame suggested, "Let us move on to a special day shall we? I want to tell you a special story.

"On this day the Melchizedeck Celestial Collective on the thirteenth dimension had decided to send a few avatars to different parts of the world to help boost the Planetary Energy Field and move forward to meet the Ascension date line.

"To the Middle East there were a small group of Star Seeds. They will be called the Essene, the Children of Light. This will be a group of teachers and healers comprised of both male priests and female priestess. They will be the purest spiritual people to walk the Earth. The souls of these new beings come directly from the Celestial Brilliance. Their essence is full of love.

"They will reintroduce to humanity the original teaching of the power of love, the One Source of Life, and sacred rites to Ascension. Through them many damaged souls will be saved. They will continue what Ahken's mission was cut short and expand the Ascension Program worldwide. Moreover, there will be others of the same persuasion. They will be sent to the Middle East and Far East countries. They will be known by other names easily understood by the local cultures. There will be many angels to walk the Earth. All these again is to bring balance."

And so it happened. Sprkle saw on the holographic record of the work of the Essene people. They resided up on a hill away from the maddening crowd. Their living quarters and temples were simple and basic. They wore linen garment, mostly white. Same style for men and women. Their food was mostly bread and vegetables and sometimes fish. Male and female married and were encouraged to have children. However, the choice of marriage was flexible. Some opted to stay single throughout their lives especially those who travel much to the outside world to teach.

He also noticed that there were small pockets of people mostly spiritual teachers and healers doing wonderful things in different parts of the globe. And then Purple Flame appeared.

"My dear, there are myriads of time lines and parallel worlds, and I know that you want to know everything, which is not possible at this point in time without blowing your mind up with confusion. I suggest you pay attention to one line at a time.

"Since we are covering the Essene topic, therefore we focus on the time line of the Middle East in particular Jerusalem and Egypt. These places were under the rule of the Roman Empire. The Roman were self-serving, corrupt, and cruel to the local populace, who were very unhappy. They organized small occasional revolts and unrest with the intention of booting out the oppressive foreign devils, but without success. This whole area was a boiling point of deep hatred and constant violence.

"Now here is a turning point. A plan was to send an avatar of Light of the highest calibre ever sent to Earth. This particular celestial being belongs to a titanic collective of Beings. They are pure light/love, pure music, pure life force. This superpower resides within the twelve dimension. They never incarnate, never taken a form of any kind. Their pastime is mostly to create worlds and universe with Life Force Energy.

"Remember I told you about Ascension Time Line? Well, there is a date we have to meet, so this is crucial time and crucial action is called for. Right now the etheric body of Earth is vibrating at a low level due to the clutch of the dark energy net surrounding her. Centuries of war and destruction is pulling the planet and its people down to hell. There is a necessity to break this net before anything else could be done. The whole process is very complex and needs centuries if not millennia to complete, but the initial work has to be done now.

"So one celestial being of the twelfth dimension was chosen and agreed to incarnate for the first time on Earth to do one thing only and that was to save the planet and as many of her children as possible by raising their vibration.

"He will singlehandedly reestablish and activate the Healing Zone for damaged souls and the multidimensional portals secretly built in various parts of the world so that Earth's planetary field will be ready to meet the time line in the future.

"The plan is to create a force within the planet powerful enough to open a channel so that it can receive another high frequency energy band sent down from space to break and shatter the menacing dark energy net once and for all.

"This special avatar will be a male, and he will be born on Earth in the year 12 BC. In order to do what needed to be done, it was necessary for him to take on a physical body. His birth, even though was the grandest occasion ever, it was covered with the utmost secrecy in order to guarantee his survival and thereafter his mission. It was dangerous time. If the Fallen Angel and the local religious leaders even caught wind of his existence, they will do everything to hunt him and kill him."

"Will he have a father and a mother like a normal human being?" Sprkle asked with pure innocence.

"Well, no. You might call it an immaculate conception because no human male biological semen was needed. His DNA imprint was that of celestial level, not human. He did not need a human father that would be too low a vibration."

"That would be strange. How was it done?"

"First of all a female was chosen for the assignment. She was born and raised by an Essene family, an extension of the Brotherhood of Light. She was pure, young, beautiful, and groomed to be the future high priestess and leader of the Essene tribe. She was duly contacted by the angels and asked for her approval of the plan that would change her life forever. She then agreed to be miraculously impregnated and will carry the pregnancy to full term and give birth to a very special child. A spouse would be chosen for her later, and he would be the foster father of the child.

"The following procedure will be for the avatar to slow down his vibration to match that of the future mother. When the time was right, he turned his personal energy field into a speck of light. This light will be inserted into the womb to activate the female egg of the mother. Thereafter, the pregnancy began. The whole operation was very quick and totally painless, and the mother thought that she just had a dream.

"Nine months later a baby boy was born. Let us call him J-12. The year was 12 BC. Three months later he was taken secretly by the high priest of Ur to a secret temple in Egypt.

"Years passed, and so undiscovered and undetected, he was raised and trained and given the maps and codes to activate the secret portals in Egypt, the Himalayan Valleys, Tibet, the Far East and other deep underground places as well.

"J-12 spent many years travelling in the Eastern nations, learning their colourful cultures. He mainly communicated with religious teachers, priests, and lamas. He was a teachers' teacher. He never wrote anything down, but many books were written by his students to remember his words of wisdom.

"His main mission was really to balance the vibrational frequencies of all the multidimensional portals in secret places in different areas of the world.

"Raising the Planetary Force Field of the whole planet Earth was the all-important groundwork that was the necessary first step.

"Next will depend on the human beings incarnate. Their Personal Energy Field vibration have to be lifted high enough to match the Planetary Force Field in order to work. You remember I told you before that all earthlings Energy Field are interconnected with the Planetary Field. Well, one cannot exist without the other. At the very least there have to be a minimum number of human being who possess high vibration to match up. Even so the whole process is very intricate, complex, and delicate.

"Now you understand what I mean that in order for Earth/Terra to meet the Ascension Time Line much work needs to be done yet?

"When it was said that a saviour of the world would come and live among Man, as predicted by earlier ancient prophets, most people, at a later date, misunderstood that this saviour meant J-9, who was more visible and popular at the time; but in fact, it was J-12 that the wise prophets knew to be closer to the truth.”

“Wow! Tell me more.”

“When his mission was over and done, he dematerialized his physical body, released his soul, and went back Home in full accomplishment and glory.”

“Wow, that is the way. I want to be like him one day. This is very inspirational.”

“Meanwhile, something else happened. Another avatar was chosen and sent to incarnate on Earth.”

“Another one? Why? Who was he?”

“Well, patience, my dear. This one was different. This avatar was chosen from the ninth dimension, the realm of the collective angelic Beings called the Christ. So let’s call him J-9 the Christ. He was chosen mainly to work among the Middle Eastern area, and he would be a people’s man. Unlike J-12 who worked secretly involving portals and star gates and moved mostly among religious temples in the East, J-9 would be involved mostly with raising the vibration of the multitude, the mass population, the common people, the ‘lost lambs’ so to speak.

“The procedure for the conception and pregnancy for this new avatar was mostly the same as the last one. This time a young woman was chosen from the Jewish/Hebrew stock. Again a man was chosen to be the spouse for the young lady and the foster father of the new baby.

“J-9 was born in the year 7 BC (five years younger than J-12) to a Jewish Hebrew family. He was raised learning the Jewish faith as well as the Essene way. When he was twelve years old, he started to travel with his rich uncle, the brother of his mother. From then on he loved to travel. “He graduated from the Essene school as a full-fledged high priest of the Brotherhood of Light. Since he was a specially chosen one, he knew what his ministry was going to be. He was to be a travelling teacher of Love and the Law of One.

“At age twenty, he stood a head taller than most men. He was slim and strong, elegant in his movement. He had fair skin and auburn hair with a light reddish tint. His eyes were the biggest attraction of all. He had beautiful bright-blue eyes that exude a magnetic power and deep love. Everyone that looked at his eyes, whether men, women or children and even animals, would fall in love with him. He had a powerful charismatic aura about him that was almost hypnotic. Whenever he spoke, throng of people would listen attentively and would follow him like bees to honey everywhere he went.

"He was a great teacher and healer as well. His travel would bring him all over the Middle Easter area, through the Mediterranean Sea to Greece, Syria, Persia, and so on. Later on to the West, he would cover Rome, France, and as far as England.

"Thousands of people were touched and healed by him through the years. Thus, his ministry was to raise vibration of the souls of the people. He was constantly travelling abroad, going as far and as wide as possible, reaching many different races and classes of humanity.

"His popularity in the Hebrew community caught the attention of the local Jewish high priests. They saw him as a threat to their control of their flock for they were leaving their temple to follow J-9.

"The temple preached fear and demanded offering and sacrifices for salvation. J-9 demanded nothing from them. He talked about the following:

- Freedom, joy, equality of men and women, salvation was free for all, no sacrifice.
- His way to salvation was easy to follow and attain. There was no need to be able to read big books. Even the illiterate could follow and therefore be saved.
- His technique was just love and respect oneself and love others as oneself. Anyone can do this, even children.
- The poor and the sick would be the first to go to Heaven. The Power is in each person, men, women and children alike, no need temple, no need of priests, the Kingdom of God is within each one and can be reached directly.
- Just knock and the Door of Heaven will open. Ask and God will response.
- God does not demand gold and silver. The Way to God is only love, unconditional love.

He used simple words and stories to convey deep spiritual meaning. His teaching was like music to the ears of the multitude of ordinary people especially the destitute.

"Unlike the temples where people needed to travel far to go to, J-9 went to the people. He would go to the fishing villages to talk to the fishermen. He would visit farms to talk to the farmers. He would go to the hills and gardens where people were working or resting. He reached out to the community. He brought his teaching to the homes of the rich and the poor. He would preach and heal anyone, anywhere, and anytime. He often travels to foreign countries to give blessings and baptism to all the Jewish diaspora and those that were deemed unclean, therefore rejected by the Temple.

"The Jewish priests sent spies to follow him, hoping to find some excuse to stop him by putting him in prison. As time went by, they could not find any fault in J-9's action. They were getting more and more alarmed as the numbers of followers grew from dozens to hundreds and then to thousands very quickly. He was becoming a very powerful leader. The threat that he posed to their establishment, not to mention their fast decreasing income, was becoming too real.

"It was decided among the councils of the Jewish religion that J-9 had to be stopped and soon. The man had to be eliminated, no less. They waited until he returned to his hometown and then to capture him first and then invent some excuses later to kill him.

"J-9 was alerted by one of his disciples and managed to escape. It was necessary for him to continue his mission of peace. He could not be stopped and harmed in any way. He had to carry his life mission of teaching and healing to the end of his term. He was after all a 9D angelic avatar. He did not come to Earth to be tortured and killed by human. He came to save them."

"Meanwhile, a drama was invented by his disciples. A man was chosen to replace J-9 to go through the trials and the persecution. He agreed to take part in this in order to avert the attention of the authority to pursue J-9, whom he loved and revered. It would be an honour for him to be chosen. Angels were called in to help, and the man suffered minimum of pain after having ingested special herbs to numb his senses. After the crucifixion, he was rescued from the cave alive and brought to heal in a safe place where he lived in peace and prosperity and died at the ripe old age of sixty."

"What happen to J-9? Did escape alone or with others? Where did he go?" "So many questions! Well, remember his rich uncle? Well, he was a trader and he owned many ships. His uncle took J-9, his wife, their children, his mother, and his brothers and sisters.”

“His wife? When did he get married and to whom? How many children did he have?”

“So many questions! He got married at the age of thirty-three with a close companion called Mary. She was originally from Egypt. She was trained there by the school of the Urtite priests. In terms of religious and spiritual knowledge, she was no less than J-9. She had her own group of followers, both male and female. She would later on set up schools of her own to continue the teaching J-9 left behind.

“As a human male, one of the finest specie, I must add, J-9 fathered two children. It was necessary for him to start the seeding of a pure blood line of high vibration. He would have many grandchildren. His bloodline continued to the modern time.

“Going back to the story. The entourage sailed through the Mediterranean Sea and landed in southern France. They sailed along the river inland and settled somewhere in the Provence area. When everything was set up, sometime later J-9 left the family to continue his ministry in Rome. When his mission was completed at age thirty-nine, J-9 dematerialized his physical body, turned into pure light, and returned his consciousness to the Christ realm. Once home, he was greeted with the most glorious welcome.”

“Did he leave any books or written documents?”

“During his ministry J-9 did some translation of the original spiritual text into the Hebrew language, but these were lost and not yet found. Maybe it was not yet time to reveal them. He did not write anything about himself. In any case, through his dispensations, he laid down the foundation for both the Jewish and Christian faith. Others wrote about him, unfortunately, in time even these were twisted and corrupted.”

“What a wonderful story, thank you, my dear teacher. Was it all true?” “It is up to you what you choose to believe. So much for now, my dear one.” *Poof!* Purple Flame was gone.

CHAPTER 6

CE - THE CURRENT ERA

The Rise of Empires

Sprkle moved the time forward and observed.

As the Wheel of Fortune turned once again, the ugly head of darkness was rising.

It was time for the empire builders to come forward. This was the time of integration of small and weak kingdoms to be joined as one. It was time of the clash of titans. The strong will rule, and the weak will perish. This was the time for the birth of emperors. No more small kings.

After the fall of the empire of Alexander, a new one was growing in Rome. This was even more powerful and lasted longer than ever before. It went from 100 to 380 CE. At its height the Roman Empire spread from Rome, Italy, to the north to the British Isles, to the east to Byzantine, to the south to Egypt and North Africa.

Their rulers, even though not dynastic, did have a continuous line of men who rose to the top position through shear military might or through cunning and murderous means.

As rulers the Roman were advance military strategists with the latest engineering technique and the best possible weapons for that era; but they also left a legacy of harsh cold tyranny, ruthlessness, and blood thirsty atrocities.

The Roman was famous for their blood sport. The most horrific killings were displayed in their huge arena built for thousands. Human slaves were forced to fight to the death among themselves. As if not enough, they later on introduced large animals like hungry lions and tigers to the arena. Thousands of spectators would roar with excitement and elation as they watched the human bodies being torn apart and their flesh and blood flung to the air in all direction.

This was done just for fun and entertainment.

Seeing this, Sprkle was disgusted and revolted. He said to himself, "One thing is killing on the battlefield for a cause, but torture for fun? Where has human morality gone to?"

He moved time forward to the fall of the Roman Empire. Even though it was gradual, it started with many defeated battles and was eventually over by around 370 CE.

He stayed on Europe, and after about two hundred years, he witnessed another horrific scene. There was vast spread of a disease called the bubonic plague. Millions died in the most excruciating pain and prolonged suffering.

Europe was covered with darkness, utmost poverty, filth, sorrow, despair, helplessness, and hopelessness.

Then Sprkle changed his view to another area on the Record.

He looked toward the East. He saw Tang Dynasty in China. Despite of skirmishes and small conflicts, mainly in the border area, the Chinese Dragon Empire was mainly peaceful and prosperous. They were trading with different nations in the East.

It was a time of beautiful silk, silver, gold, art, and new creation of lacquer wares, porcelain, and so forth. Many scholars and poets appeared during this time. The young emperors of the beginning period of the Tang Dynasty were open-minded and willing to explore the territories beyond their border.

A trading land route to the west called the new Silk Road was established. Through this new venture, he obtained a detailed map of the terrain from the Chinese capital, Lo Yeung, to India. With this first-hand information, it would facilitate his future campaign. Also during this period Buddhism was introduced to China.

About the same time in the Middle East, a new sage was initiated by the angels. He was Muhammad. Through the guidance of the Celestial Beings, he wrote a book of divine grace called the Qur'an. Next he started a new religion called Islam.

Sprkle asked his teacher, "What is this new teaching?"

Purple Flame explained, "This teaching was not new. This was the old text of the Law of One. This teaching was as old as time, but often the human mind forgets and lead their lives astray.

"Through Muhammad thousands were reconverted to the Law of One. Islam spread like a fresh wind from heaven all over the desert land of the Middle East, touching hearts and opened minds. Soon after the establishment of the Islam religion, a military campaign was organized to take Jerusalem, which they claimed to be their ancient heritage. They succeeded in 600 CE. Thereafter, the rise of the Empire of the Moors.

"Unfortunately, after Muhammad went back to heaven, two of his followers both claimed to be his successors. And from then on these two Islamic factions were at war with each other, killing in the name of the one God that they both believed in."

Sprkle exclaimed, "This is insane!" He sighed, and he moved his attention to somewhere else.

He saw the invasion of the Vikings who went from the Scandinavian area via the maritime route to the British Isles and beyond. Another scene of violence.

The Vikings were looking for food and warmer climate where they could plant, farm, and settle. Unfortunately, they did this the wrong way. They, killed, plunder, stole, rape, and burnt their way through.

Moving time forward, and Jerusalem was on fire. He saw battles between white men on horseback wearing chainmail and white garment with a big red cross wielding big straight swords against the tan-coloured men with turban, the Turks, wielding big curved swords.

Sprkle then understood that this was another battle for the holiest of holy land, Jerusalem, where three religious faith claimed to belong to their only God.

Sprkle said to himself, "Another fight in the name of God. Why are they doing this? Did they not receive the same teachings through their holy books, which clearly stated the Universal Presence of the One Creator? Are we not all brothers and sisters? If we love our God should we not also love each other too? What a waste of life. I am not going to waste my time watching these silly people."

He turned his attention to another timeline.

On the other side of the globe. Sprkle saw the massive horse riding nomadic tribe called the Mongols. The time was around 1260 CE. Another empire builder, the Mongolian Empire. Like wild fire, they rode, killed and plundered their way from the border of China westward to Russia, Persia, and all the way to Europe. Later on they turned their sight to the East and went to China.

This was a dynastic clan. Their reign of terror was long and enduring. They were rough, physical, and almost no culture, no religion, mostly nomadic. So every nation that they conquered they would try to settle and assimilate the local culture and the way of life of the people. As the empire was vast, covering many different nations, therefore many Mongolian settled in all these places and became multinationals. After many mix marriages and the following generations, the Mongols had lost their original nomadic heritage, except those who never left their land.

Their very long reign ended in 1640.

Back to Europe. After another terrible bout of disease and widespread plague called the Black Death, Europe was on the rise again.

This time a new birth.

It was peace time, the golden age of new artistic creation of all kinds— in architecture, in fashion, sculptures, paintings. New ships and trading routes opened, and people were prosperous and adventurous.

A glorious new birth in the form of the Renaissance.

Sprkle learned that after the breaking up of the Roman Empire, all the previous small countries resumed to their old pattern of kings and feudal landlords.

Sprkle also noticed that all the beautiful things about the Renaissance were only happening in the small circles of people. They were the monarchies of Europe, the aristocracies, and the rich big traders.

Then there was the Roman Catholic Church, its leader was called the pope, who claimed to be divine, to be the sole representative of God, therefore indisputably the highest spiritual power of the world.

This establishment comprised of thousands of men and women whose mission were to preach the dogma and convert people. Their teaching is that all human beings are sinners. Their souls are soiled because of the sins of Adam and Eve against God. Only the Church has the power to cleanse those souls who will go to heaven if they surrender all to the Church or go to everlasting fire and suffering in hell if they do not. There is no way out, no reincarnation to make amend. They call their followers their flock of sheep, and they do treat them accordingly. The pope is their shepherd. This church demanded offering in the form of gold, silver, land and slaves. Slaves are called faithful sheep and it is an honour to war to kill and to be killed for the Church.

Later on in time, The Church had transformed itself into a political entity called the Vatican, which operate as a nation within a nation of Italy. The pope, its king and divine being in one man.

The Vatican operated very closely with the royal courts in Europe. There was a time it was so rich and powerful that it declared that the pope, a divine manifestation of God should have the power to enthrone or dethrone kings or queens. Only those recognized by the Vatican were declared legitimate, and those not in line with this policy would be banished and even attacked and destroyed by its army.

The Vatican wielded holy terror in Europe among the rich and poor alike. This was the Inquisition. Witch hunting was the order of the day, and the most excruciating torture was practiced especially for women and all those who were deemed to be straying from their faith. Many died in horrific and cruel atrocities. This was one of the ways to secure power over the mind of souls.

Following the time line of this establishment, Sprkle learned that this people were actually the descendants of the Annunak, the ancient Sumerian elite, later on the Egyptian Brotherhood of the Serpent. They just adopted a new façade and new name, but underneath their skin they were the same beings. Even their spiritual practice is very similar.

The Vatican and the Crowns of Europe were the most powerful people in the world during this period. They built huge castles and palaces and surrounded themselves with splendour behind high walls. With every conquest, they would claim ownership of the land, the people, the farms and stock. The elite separate themselves from the population who were generally poor and defenceless.

The mortality rate of the common people was very high.

There was a time when the sheer weight of oppression, desperate poverty, constant death and famine among the masses was too much to bear; and when there was nothing else to lose but life itself, human fought back.

The will to live, to survive, is inherent to all human beings. So when life condition had become so bad that even that small candle light within the human soul is about to be extinguished and no alternative path to be found, people rise up.

And so widespread revolt occurred, the poor against the rich. Kitchen knives, guns, famer's forks, anything that could hurt and kill was being implemented and turned into weapons. Many royal heads rolled. From killing for food later on became killing for killing's sake. Utter madness descended upon the people. This went on for many years.

When the rivers of water became rivers of blood and the energy for violence was almost exhausted, a young man appeared among the chaos. He was given financial support to rebuild. He was French; and so armed with money, youth, and ambition, he started a military campaign that resulted some years later as an empire. He then crowned himself emperor. The French empire was the last of the European one-man-emperor paradigm. From then on the European countries will rearranged themselves and a new play began.

Sprkle moved time forward, and he saw a fleet of sailing ships sailing from Europe across the Atlantic Ocean towards the big land on the other side.

Next, he saw that they landed on the southern area and soon what followed was the all familiar scene of battle, bloodbath, conquest, firearms against bows and arrows, new disease descended among the native with no immune defence. It was just disaster and total ethnic cleaning.

On the northern part of the big land, the same pattern repeated itself.

More ships and men landed and the rest is history.

Sprkle named them the Elite Group. The kings and nobles had military power, the rich traders and bankers had wealth, the Vatican had religious power. Together there was little they could not accomplish in this world. The many conquests and colonization of the land beyond the Atlantic Ocean, which they named the North and South Americas, Africa, and other nations had brought to the Elite Group enormous new land mass and unimaginable wealth. All the while the kings collected slaves of the physical bodies and the Vatican practised slavery of souls.

Now the Elite Group extended their sight to the whole world.

At this point in time Sprkle had some questions, "Teacher, all this building up of power and wealth by this Elite Group to what purpose? What do they really want? Why are most human seem to be numb and weak? Why are they following all those false prophets and priests whom they call fathers and willing to offer not only their very life, but also that of their families, especially their children? I have so many questions in my mind, please help."

Purple Flame explained, "All these happenings are pointing to one target and that is the Final Battle, the End Game, for the full control of the galactic star gates. My dear, there is a much bigger game being played in which the little planet Earth is just one part of. The Elite Group and all those other religious and political groups are just puppets on strings. Above them there are their lords and controllers.

"I can see that you are perplexed and somewhat confused. Well, I will tell you what you need to know in due time. This is an extremely complex issue, and you have reached the most critical point."

"Yes, Teacher. Having followed the Earth's time line in the holographic record, it had indeed very clearly showed a pattern of war and peace, era of horrific violence and darkness followed by golden era of light and high spiritual awareness. Indeed, it seems like a wheel going up and down and up again.

"Since I was mainly interested in the story of the blue planet, I am just concerned about this and fail to see the big picture as you mentioned. What have I missed then, please enlighten."

"All in good time, my dear."

"I am wondering if I could reincarnate once more to learn the lesson of the modern man in modern time."

"I think it is worth considering, because the 1900s, the last century of the first millennia and the turning point of another era, another stage of the astrological clock, the Age of Aquarius, the Age of Light. This is indeed very interesting time.

"I can see that serious mishaps are looming in front, and there will be hard times ahead. Remember the Wheel? It has to reach the lowest point, the darkest of hour, when everything is lost, stone-cold dead, then it can start to move upward.

"My dear, Earth is about to reach this point. Do you still want to go? This is not going to be a pleasant journey, but if you take up this challenge, you would indeed learn much and raise your soul vibration further. You would also be a channel of positive energy during this critical time. Let me know when you have made your decision."

"Of course, whenever Mother Earth call, I will be there for her. I love her so much. I can go any time."

"Wait, my dear. We must not rush into action. First, we must think when and where it is best for you to go. Meanwhile, would you like to see what is happening right at the beginning of 1900?"

"Yes, you are right, Teacher. Let me see more, and we will talk later."

The Contemporary Time Line

It was July 1914. Sprkle saw in Europe various countries were amassing fire power. They drew a line between opposite sides like a chessboard, and they were firing at each other. Started with a few countries at first, but soon all the other countries were involved. All the countries on the eastern and the western side of the globe were at war. The Earthlings called it World War I.

Millions died. It was short though, it only lasted for four years.

After this war, the winning side were more wealthy and powerful than before. The Elite Group now regroup themselves and divided among themselves the spoils of the wars. This new way of creating wealth wet their appetite. The ugly head of greed rose and preparation for a next round was quickly put together.

Yes, over seventy million died. That was only on official record, but actually many more deaths were hidden. Those who died were the fortunate ones. Those who were severely injured, those whose homes were destroyed, those whose loved ones were taken away and never returned or returned as zombies, those who had lost all their basic survival means, these were worse off.

Prolonged misery is very heavy for the soul.

The refugee camps were full of people living in dire, dismal conditions. They would kill for just a cup of warm watery soup in the cold, bleak winter.

Sprkle saw the Elite Group, rich and fat in their grand palaces, shut off from the common people with high walls. They were saying, "Making tanks, guns, bombs and selling them for war makes money. We need to double, or triple, production and get new brains to create bigger bombs, faster tanks and better fighter planes. This is great fun. To hell with the people. The more people die the better for us. Easier to control and manipulate. They are all our slaves anyway. Obey us or perish. This is the name of the game. Hell, we want another world war."

And so their wish came true. The next one was quick, only took twenty-one years and they got another war. They call it World War II.

And they said, "Hell, we want this one to be bigger, more deadly than ever, we want every single country from the far west to the far east and from the North Pole to the South Pole. No one will be spared. We want the best brains, the best technologies, the best bomb. If we could achieve instant annihilation, it would be best."

Again, Sprkle saw that their wish came true. He was horrified to see that scientists had a blueprint plan to build the deadliest bomb—the atomic bomb. He knew what this meant.

Sprkle, suddenly decided that he would like to reincarnate in this period. It was going to be challenging to say the least, but he wanted to be a part of this extraordinary time. This time he wanted to experience a man of the yellow race. He saw that Japan was invading China. He did not want to be the aggressor. He wanted to be in China, the receiving end. He asked Purple Flame, "How about a Chinese male during the Sino-Japanese war and following that the Chinese civil war. What do you think?"

"Hmm, there will certainly be a lot of lessons on courage and fear, I would say, not to mention further lessons on endurance and perseverance. You are sure about this, my dear?"

"Yes, I am determined. You said that this is interesting time, so this little soul likes to experience interesting time. You know me."

"All right then. An interesting life line will be arranged for you. As you well know that all life lines are not etched in stones, so the software program there can be changed according to your choice of actions during your sojourn in this reality. You may or may not accomplish what you set out originally. In any case, it is worth a try."

And so Sprkle and Purple Flame worked out a general plan with a small group of souls, and when all were in agreement, it was time for manifestation and a new journey for Sprkle began.

CHAPTER 7

THE SOJOURN IN CHINA

The First Seven Years

The date was September 26, 1893, China. A baby boy was born with the name Chan Ah Man to a Chinese family. His parents were poor rural farmers who lived on a small plot of land rented from a rich landlord. They grew vegetables and owned one buffalo, some chicken and ducks. They kept what they needed for food, and the rest they sold to pay rent. They had to work very hard to keep up with the yearly production; otherwise, they would not be able to pay rent.

When the weather was bad and production low, after deducting rent and government tax, there was very little money left for the family; and during this period, they would have less to eat. More often than not, one dish of preserved vegetables, some beans, a couple of chicken eggs, and white rice were to be shared by the family of six.

Chan Ah Man had two elder brothers and one elder sister. They all helped out with the daily chores at the farm, and they take their turn to look after him. For the first two months after he was born, Ma Ma would give him her milk. It was nice, and he looked forward to this very much. He would feel so much love and protection from being held in her bosom; and the food from her body was so warm, so good, and satisfying.

On the third month, things changed. Ma Ma no longer gave him her milk. Instead, he was given a kind of rice drink from a broken bowl, which was definitely not the same as her warm bosom, and the rice thing was much less satisfying. But at least it stopped the hunger, so he did not protest much.

Later on, Ah Man would come to learn that there had been a bad harvest that year and everybody in the family had such a strict food rationing that Ma Ma became undernourished and therefore could no longer produce milk in her body. Following this bad year, a better one came and so the family more or less survived. Sometimes there would be more food on the table, sometimes less.

Years passed, and soon Ah Man was five years old. This year he would see his elder brother, Ah Long, leaving the family to a faraway land they called the Golden Mountain. He would go as labourer to earn more money for the family.

After he left Ah Man would have more work to do on the farm.

Two years later, when he was seven years old, another change in the family came. His sister, Ah Jan, was married to a man whose family lived in the next village some ten miles away.

I will not see her very often from now on, he thought. *Probably never. The next village is like another world. How I can travel so far?*

Ah Man felt very sad because he was very close to this sister, who was his playmate and constant companion when Ma Ma was always busy. Ah Jan was a second mother to him, protecting him from harmful elements and taught him the correct way to complete his daily chores in the farm, like feeding the chicken and ducks and collecting eggs carefully. She helped him with work that was too heavy or difficult for him. She cuddled him and soothed his fears when he had bad dreams. She held him close in her arms during thunderstorms and many fearful nights.

One day he watched her getting dressed in a red costume. Even her head was covered with a piece of red cloth. Then she was taken away by some strangers. He felt like his little heart was broken. He cried so much that he could not sleep for many nights. She was the one person to whom he could reach out when there was fear and doubt, and now she was no more.

"What am I going to do?" he said to himself. "What will become of me? I cannot imagine life without my sister."

Ah Man thought about his sister and sadness overwhelmed him.

Rivers of tears flowed for many days and nights.

This was also the year that Ah Man started school. Soon autumn came, and he was ready for change.

His father called him to his side one evening after dinner, when all the washing and cleaning had been done. He told Ah Man that if he was willing to learn to read and write, the family could save enough money to pay for his schooling. His father said that since he was the youngest and his other brothers were working and saving, they would like to see at least one member of the family acquire an education and that one day, hopefully, he would lift the whole family from poverty. Ah Man was their only hope for a better future.

The boy of seven could not understand much about hope or future, but he was looking forward to go off somewhere so that he could just get away from the tending of pigs, ducks, and chickens all day long. He would be happy to go to school, he told his father. And so it was decided unanimously.

Primary School

On the first day of school, his father woke Ah Man very early, and after brushing his teeth and washing his face, his father produced a new clean white shirt and a new pair of blue trousers. He told him that this was his school uniform and that he should wear it to school every day but to be mindful to keep the clothes clean because they were the only ones he would ever get.

The boy was elated. He had never seen new clothes before, especially ones that were so white and fit him so perfectly and bought for him only. He usually wore his brother's old clothes and they were old and baggy and all the colours were faded from years of washing.

"Hmm, this is a new beginning," Ah Man told himself. "This is exciting. I wonder what school is like. This is a new adventure."

His father brought him to school on the first day, and thereafter, he had to go alone. The school was in a nearby village, which was much bigger compared to their own village. He had to walk for about an hour to school and back. He did not mind because this was like an adventure for him.

He walked along rice fields, gardens, and vegetable farms every day, observing the life in the surrounding neighbourhood. He looked at the animals; the fish in the fish ponds; and the plants; the rice fields; and people working, moving, interacting, buying, selling, feeding, etc. Every day, along this little journey of his, there would always be one thing or other that Ah Man liked to poke his curious nose into. There was so much to see and learn.

The school was a small building with many rooms, and he and some thirty children, all boys, occupied one big room. Everything in this school seemed to be very old. The building, all the tables and chairs, and most of the books were all used and tattered.

The teacher, Wong Lao Shi, was a kind, middle-aged man. He greeted the new batch of children warmly and said that he would be their teacher for the next six years. He was the only teacher in this school.

Under his guidance and teaching, Ah Man learned how to read, and from then on he discovered a great hunger for knowledge. He read every book that was given to him and was always asking for more. He became a good student, passing every test and examination with flying colours. His parents were proud of him and continued to save money to support his schooling.

During his primary school years, life was generally routine and uneventful.

One day Ah Man woke up especially early because that day was primary school graduation, the last day in school.

Ah Man felt sad when it was time to say goodbye to all his friends, but especially to Wong Lau Shi, his second father, his beloved teacher, and his best friend. He had learned much during these years; and now, even though he was sad to leave, he was also looking forward to change. He was ready to move on into something new, a new environment, new adventure. He was becoming restless and very curious about the world beyond the villages.

Before he left school, Wong Lau Shi handed him a letter of recommendation should he plan to go to high school.

He went home and planned to discuss with his father the possibility of further studies. He knew that there was only one high school in the city, which was quite far away. This meant leaving home and staying in the city. He considered the cost of the school fees, which would be much higher, and also the extra food and boarding fees. Could the family afford this?

There were thousands of students within the city itself and the surrounding villages all trying to get into this school. The standard was high, and the competition fierce. Was Ah Man's grade good enough? Could he stand a slim chance to squeeze himself through the cracks into this famous school? Most city students were usually better prepared than village folks.

Somehow, Wong Lao Shi thought very highly of Ah Man's abilities and told him he was confident that he could at least have a slim chance. His letter highly recommended him and highlighted all his past good works. He suggested that he should at least give it a try, and he would personally help him to prepare for his entrance examination. Ah Man, thus encouraged, was determined to try; but he first must face his father. After reading Wong Lao Shi's letter and having heard Ah Man's plea,

his father was very quiet. In the past two years, due to bad weather, the harvest had been bad. After paying government tax and land rental, the remaining production was barely enough to feed the family. There was some money they had saved up from previous good years, but the sum was small and not enough even to pay the school fees let alone his food and lodging.

After thinking deeply for a long while, his father told Ah Man that he needed more time to think about this matter. He would also write to his elder brother, Ah Tong in the Golden Mountain country, to ask for his help.

Well, there was nothing Ah Man could do except wait. He had a heavy heart at the thought of bringing an extra burden to the family; but at the same time he felt this burning fire inside for more knowledge, for new adventures, new experience.

He needed to soar high. He needed to move away from this poverty, this endless struggle with little or no reward. He needed to go and see what lay on the other side of the "mountain." He needed to change this miserable existence. He *would* bring fame, fortune, and glory to his beloved family! He *would* bring the necessary change of a better life. All eyes were on him. He could not fail, and for this reason, he needed more education.

One and half months passed. One day, a letter arrived from the Golden Mountain country far away. Father opened it with trembling hands while Ah Man bit his lips in nervous anticipation.

Father read the good news to the family. Ah Tong would get an extra job so that he would be able to support Ah Man's high school fees. Tears of joy came, and everyone in the family gave a collective sigh of relief.

Ah Man felt his knees went soft, and he knelt on the floor. Relief, joy, hope, gratitude, excitement—all these emotions rushed into him like a mighty river. He could not control himself, and he cried and cried.

Father made Ah Man promise for the two hundredth time to study hard, work hard, and pay back the money to Ah Tong one day.

That very day, dinner was a grand occasion. Apart from the normal beans and vegetables, there was one whole chicken, richly marinated with ginger and soy sauce. The last time Ah Man had seen this yummy dish with one whole chicken was two years ago.

The following two months Ah Man was very busy. He had to work and earn money for his school uniform and books. He also had to get as many books as possible to prepare for the great challenge ahead.

Through friends and friends of friends, he managed to find out the criteria for the high school entrance examination. He had to study doubly hard because he discovered that his village primary school standard was far below what was required in the city school.

He studied nonstop for six to eight hours a day. He also spent four hours a day in his part-time job. His second brother took over his farm chores to give him more time to work. His father and mother also helped. One fine morning, the whole family woke up especially early. Ma Ma prepared a more substantial breakfast than usual, and having eaten, the family went to the central bus station together to send off Ah Man. They gave him their blessings and good wishes.

"Write home as often as you can and take good care of yourself," Ma Ma said. She looked at him with as much love and tenderness a mother could give to her son. Being the youngest, he was closest to her heart.

His father patted him on his back. "Study hard and work hard. Be steadfast and be honourable," he said.

He stiffened himself and stood up straight, but his eyes were soft and tearful. Ah Man could not say anything. There was something choking on his throat. He gave a crooked smile to everyone as if to reassure them, then he lifted his bag and stepped on the bus.

High School

Ah Man arrived after a day of travelling by train and bus. The city was a totally different world to what he had been used to. He felt like he was a frog that had just jumped out of a small well. He was filled with wonder and awe at the enormous buildings lining wide streets with all kinds of shops and eateries.

There seemed to be a million bicycles moving up and down the road like rivers. There were people everywhere in the streets. He had never seen so many people in one place before. They dressed differently and even seemed to move differently, more elegant. The body structure of both men and women seemed to be more refined, very different from the muscular and labour-intensive farm folks. Ah Man felt a rush of excitement.

This is an interesting world, he thought. *Lots of possibilities.*

On school registration day, there were thousands of students. To Ah Man, they looked like a giant swarm of black bees. Next, he was directed to the registration office where the queue stretched from that point to the outside public road over a mile long. He could not see the end. It seemed to him that everything in this world was big and every queue was long. One had to compete, to fight for everything; otherwise, one would be left behind. This place was not for the weak; only the very strong could survive in such a world. Muscle was no use here; instead, intelligence and knowledge was what was required to survive in this strange city.

"I must be strong," Ah Man told himself. "I must not let my family down. I must succeed at all cost." He thought of Ma Ma, and tears of strength filled his eyes. He buckled up, straightened his back, and marched forward to the mile-long queue.

Slowly, the line snaked up toward the school entrance. Hours passed without anyone leaving for water, food, or even the toilet.

Yes, Ah Man thought, *competition is indeed fierce. But if they will not give up, then neither shall I.*

After what seemed like an eternity, he finally managed to register and left the school building exhausted and hungry. He had learned for the first time the real meaning of the words *commitment* and *perseverance*.

Today was his thirteenth birthday. The year was 1906. A couple of weeks ago he had sat for the entrance examination, which he managed to squeeze his brain and memory like never before. When he put down his pen, he knew that he had prepared well.

That morning he went early to check the result, and he jumped for joy when he saw his name on the list. He was admitted. He stood in front of the notice board and just stared at it. He felt a bit numb when the full reality sank into him. And then he cried. He cried for his father and Ma Ma. He cried for himself. This was the first step, the first important step to a new life.

He wrote a letter to his parents to announce his success at being admitted, and father wrote back to wish him well. He again reminded him to study hard and not to forget about the responsibility he bore on his shoulders.

Life in the city was very different from the slow-paced village with its wide open space and green fields. This was like an ant hill, an ant world where everyone and everything was always on the move. Irrespective of where they were going or where they were coming from, they just moved. Like ants, they marched on and on. Everyone looked busy, always doing something or going somewhere. The streets were always busy and filled with rickshaws, bicycles, and the occasional small car belonging to the super rich on their rare visits from out-of-the-world places like Shanghai or Guangzhou.

People were everywhere, walking, eating, talking, trading, goods in stalls and shops. There were big inns for the overnight travellers and luxury restaurants, as well as the many small eateries including noodle stalls and sweet snack stalls that lined the street.

In the central plaza there was a news bulletin board with daily newspapers or extra news writings from scholars and teachers or politically- minded people who wished to voice their opinion on the current affairs of the state. Here, every morning people would gather around this bulletin board to learn about the latest happenings in their city. There were government official announcements both from the local authority and from Beijing, the central Ching Government.

Most people would look anxious and walked away, head stooped and worried, because indeed there was no good news. There was never anything on this bulletin board that one could find to celebrate.

Like everybody else, Ah Man would go to the bulletin board every morning, eager to know more about the life of this city. Curiosity was his second nature, and once he had settled, he needed to dig deeper into all aspects of life there. He noticed that, despite the busy and glamorous façade, there was actually a lot of poverty, discontent, and injustice. However, more importantly, for the first time in his life he learned that his country was not what he had previously thought it was.

He was surprised to learn that there were foreign powers occupying some parts of the land as colonies and that this land was cut off from the rest of China, like a separate limb from the main body. Chinese were not allowed into this part of China. He learned that not all of China belonged to the Chinese people.

This was very puzzling to him. However, for now he would need to concentrate on his studies and work part-time whenever possible to help pay for his food and lodging in school.

So for the next three years, apart from attending school, he would have small part-time jobs such as helping in restaurants, cleaning and scrubbing, or running errands for big companies or delivering small goods from shops to people's homes, etc. He would work more during the holidays because he did not have enough money to travel back to the village.

He wrote to his family once a month to tell them about his progress and also what he had learned from the news board.

A few years passed, and during this time, Ah Man learned more about the affairs of his city and China in general. And the more he learned, the more worried he became.

He learned that the poor and discontented people were becoming more desperate and more violent as frustration and anger escalated. There were protests and demonstrations almost every day and people, mostly men, were being drafted into one party or the other and thereafter called up to fight for one cause or the other. More often than not they were like forced slaves.

There were also social and cultural changes. Some people had cut off their pigtails and wore a new kind of western-style clothing. Ah Man decided to keep his "tail" just in case the politics changed back to the old ways.

Sometimes there would be Ching police and military bossing around and roughing up people while at other times the liberal and their military men in uniforms would go around town bullying passersby and arresting anyone with the slightest suspicion.

Different factions had their own police or military force with different coloured uniforms. The political situation was very confusing, and everyone lived in fear and worries.

One day, in November 1911, Ah Man learned from the bulletin board that Beijing had declared that the Ching government was now a new republic.

Was it time to cut his hair now? Ah Man secretly wondered. He was now eighteen years old. One more year to go and he will have finished high school. After that Ah Man wanted to go to university to study journalism. During the time that he had spent running errands for different trading companies and helping in shops and restaurants, he had been exposed to people from different walks of life and overheard many supposedly secret conversations. The gossip among clients in the shops and restaurants could be quite valuable when put to use at the right time and place.

Reading the bulletin board studiously every morning, under rain or shine, enabled him to acquire a great deal of information that was not ordinarily available to most people who were illiterate. He decided that information was the key to success, and so journalism was the perfect profession to get him there. Besides, he was still as curious as a cat, always wondering what was lying on the other side of the fence.

Ah Man finished high school in the year 1912. He was nineteen years old and aiming to move to an even bigger city. Beijing was the first choice, the central seat of government, the hub of political power and also the cultural centre of China. His second choice was Shanghai, where sat the power of money and commerce.

"Nowadays, it is better to follow money," calculated the young man. "Besides, there are a lot of new political movements and new businesses and political parties mushrooming there. Every day there seems to be something changing. Now this is where the action is."

The political picture changed again very quickly that year. At the beginning of the year, Dr. Sun Yat Sen became the first president of China's New Republic. There was a big celebration, and people hoped that this would bring about peace and a new China. However, by end of the same year, he was booted out and Yuan Shi Kai promoted himself from premier to president of the Republic. Soon the last Chinese emperor, Pu Yi, was deposed marking the end of the Ching Dynasty.

Ah Man thought it was time to cut his hair for good. However, he hesitated and thought it better to wait until he got to Shanghai. The rich, the fashionable, and the powerful that moved mainstream politics were in Shanghai.

This is the future of China, Ah Man thought.

After consulting with his father about university and having learned that his big brother in America had managed to get better jobs and was sending home more money, Ah Man got the green light.

Father had taken the money earmarked to build a better house for the family to pay for his university fees, though Ah Man himself had to work to support his own food and lodging. It was the pride of the family in the village to have a son studying at the university, his father told him. In fact, Chan Ah Man was the only one that had gone so far up on the academic ladder in all the history of their village. A huge expectation sat on Ah Man's shoulder!

"Whew! Failure is not an option," he reminded himself.

Shanghai

In 1912 Ah Man moved to Shanghai and the first thing he did as soon as he arrived was to cut his pigtail. Now a new page of his life began. The competition to enter the university here was even fiercer than ever. The best students from all over the country would flock to Shanghai or Beijing for further studies. The best of the best teachers were in these two major cities. In Shanghai there was not only a rich class of people, but there was also a class they called the superrich and also the super talented. More importantly, however, they could buy their way into any school they fancied. Many of them were doing preparatory studies with their sights set on foreign countries, the most popular being America, the land of the Golden Mountain.

For small-town boy like Ah Man, he was content just to be able to learn journalism, work hard, make some money to repay his big brother, and take good care of his family. He was not planning to go anywhere.

Being an A-class student and having passed his entrance examination with excellent marks did not mean much in big Shanghai.

Hard work and talent did not get one anywhere in this town. It was all about money and/ or personal relation. Knowing who was who would get one through the door to one's desired situation in life.

One day Ah Man called in on one of his old bosses who happened to be very rich and well connected with the high society. He, fortunately, knew a friend who was willing to do him the favour of putting in a good word with the key person who sat on the committee at the university, and by a small miracle, Ah Man managed to get through the cracks and into the university.

As soon as his seat was confirmed, he wrote to inform his parents and promised to work again to pay for his living expenses. He quickly scouted for and landed on a job in a newspaper firm, as a helper at first and was later promoted to junior journalist. This job would prove to very useful in this field, facilitated his studies, and, at the same time, satisfied his ever- present hunger for information.

Life in Shanghai was dazzling. The city was a magnet for all kinds of people, from the richest to the poorest. There were also all kinds of foreigners, with different skin and hair colours that Ah Man had never encounter before.

It was a melting pot for the artists, politicians, bankers, gangsters, smugglers, traders, intellectuals, philosophers, academics, idealists, opportunists, the freedom fighters, peace lovers, and so forth.

The city was fascinating for farm boy Ah Man, who would watch the young, the rich and fashionable people moving about. He had never seen so many different kinds of vehicles that crisscrossed the roads with beautiful women and smart-looking men in Western suits. Shanghai never slept. The night scene in Shanghai was glittery, glamorous, sensual, rich, sensational, and enticing.

It was during this time that Ah Man, between multiple university projects and his hectic work at the newspaper, found time to fall in love.

A petite, porcelain-skinned, pretty Shanghainese girl caught Ah Man's eye one afternoon while he was studying in the school garden. For one moment he looked up from his book, and he thought he saw an angel, a beautiful female in the sunlight, standing in front of him. Her pale face and big bright eyes totally and utterly mesmerised the young man. That moment, Ah Man's heart stopped.

Through a friend of a friend he discovered that her name was Soong Mei Mei, that she was from a rich family, and that she was studying medicine in the same university. Luckily, the following week was the birthday party of a mutual friend, and having learned in advance that Mei Mei was going to attend, Ah Man made his move.

Being tall, strong, and handsome, as well as being well-known for being an exceptional student among his peers, Ah Man did possess a few good cards in his hands. Indeed, when he turned on his street-smart charm he was quite irresistible.

Soon he and Mei Mei became very good friends and were often seen spending time together. Though their family backgrounds were different, their political and social ideals were similar. This was a happy time for Ah Man.

Some years passed, and in 1915, he graduated at the university. After having secured a journalist license and a position in a newspaper firm, that summer Chan Ah Man made a visit back home to the village. He was twenty-two years old.

It was the first time he had returned home since he took that bus to the high school in the city ten years ago. It was going to be a very emotional meeting for him. Though he wrote to them often, he missed his Ma Ma and her home cooking. He longed to experience again that slow-paced natural lifestyle, so calm, so gentle; the night sky so dark; and the stars so bright, so beautiful, so free The open space full of green and small wild flowers, the fish ponds, the fresh air—all seemed to beckon to him, so inviting.

Well, his arrival was just as he expected—everybody cried. He was surprised to see how much his parents had aged. Ma Ma, with tears of joy on her sun-soaked face, looked frailer than he could have imagined. New members of the family greeted him. His second brother had got married to a sturdy farm girl from the next village, and they had a baby boy. They were a simple and happy family. His sister-in-law, being a farmer herself, was a great help in the daily chores.

Ma Ma seemed quite weak these days. News about his sister was good. She was well, married with three children. Her husband had left the farm and had started a business trading tobacco and cigarettes, an all-time popular commodity in this country.

Ah Man spent one full month resting, watching the stars at night, eating his favourite snacks that Ma Ma especially prepared for him and talking with the family. He also entertained all the neighbours who came to the house almost every night to congratulate him on his success in the university and his crowning achievement of securing a job in Shanghai, the city of dreams. They wanted to learn everything about city life, and the farm boy turned city boy patiently told them all the stories he knew.

These people are all family, my people, my tribe. I grew up with them. So often we used to share food when production was low and everybody was hungry. Now I am looking at their simple and innocent faces, and they warm my heart, Ah Man thought.

Even though the farm production was steady, the rent and government tax kept increasing and as a result, there was still not enough food for the growing family. It was only the combined money received from America and Ah Man's monthly salary from Shanghai that kept the family afloat.

There was talk about building a new house, with a separate section for his second brother's family, but this would have to wait. The political situation was unstable, affecting agriculture and economic life in general. Even remote villages were not spared.

Good time flew by too quickly. With a heavy heart, Ah Man said goodbye. It was particularly difficult to part with his mother. He felt sad and worried that he may not see her again. For one long moment mother and son locked eyes, which filled with tears. No words came, only conversing through their feelings, with love reaching deep into each other's hearts.

Time stopped while this deep emotional communication lasted. During this moment, something awakened inside Ah Man, a memory of wonderment and love far, far away and long ago. It was faint, but it was there, like a small flickering light. He could not recall where this memory came from.

Ah Man tore himself off, turned his back, hiding his painful face soaked in tears and jumped on the dusty bus that was waiting for him.

First Taste of Politics and a Broken Heart

May 4, 1919, the day that changed Ah Man for the rest of his life. He was twenty-five years old. With full consciousness, he allowed himself to be sucked into the escalating political whirlwind that had been stirring for the past decade. As the Ching Court was declining in power, chaos and violence was increasing. The long-dormant Chinese Dragon was stirring, and soon the full extent of its wrath would rock and shake China to its very core and stun the rest of the whole world.

That fateful morning he joined the group uprising in protest of Yuan Shi Kai government's agreement to sell off the Qingdao area to Japan. This was his first taste of political experience. There was a passion in his heart, and what was more, Mei Mei was also by his side, feeding him courage and energy. They were both totally agreeable and stood on the same side of the fence in all political and social issues.

From then on he spent more and more time in group discussions over the increasing chaotic political situation in his country. More street protests and writing propaganda leaflets filled his days. Through his newspaper job, he managed to acquire information not available to most people, gaining him a respectable position in his political group.

It pained him to learn how weak his country and people had become.

He thought about his poor family and the millions like them.

When would they be free from the landowners and the blood-sucking corrupt government suppression? When would they be fed properly? These and many more questions pushed him to the idea of land reform and the equal distribution of wealth throughout society.

In 1921 the leftist group in Shanghai formed an official political party. Ah Man signed in as a member with pride and total conviction.

In1925 Sun Yat Sen died, and shortly afterwards, Yuan Shi Kai declared himself president. However, he could only control a small area around Beijing.

From then on gun power ruled the day. Provincial warlords with military might mushroomed overnight and began to carve up the land in different provinces, cities and villages and held them hostage, like little kingdoms. The northern area of Manchuria, which had been colonised by Russia, became Manchuguo under Japan. And China eventually became totally fragmented with no central government. In effect, it was a failed state.

During the next two years, Ah Man would travel extensively to write stories about the actual happenings. Province by province he would go, talking to people— professionals, farmers, students, local government officials, etc. For months he would be on the road by foot, by bus, by ox cart, by boat, and occasionally by train.

Everywhere he went he learned about the chaotic political situation, the corruption of the military, widespread poverty, torture, false arrests, and rampant killings of civilians by cruel warlords. He felt sick and disheartened, and he was often depressed by the hopelessness of it all. Little did he know that the most turbulent times were yet to come. It was going to get much worse before it got better.

Also during this time, as if his experiences were not depressive enough, he received a letter from Mei Mei. Her parents were sending her to America to further her studies of medicine. Also, it had become apparent to her father that China was not a safe place to live anymore, and the family was preparing to migrate to America for good.

She loved China, she wrote, and was still very concerned about the current situation. She was leaving with a much sadness and hoped to return one day in the future but did not know when that might be. She hoped that his contribution for a better tomorrow would be successful. She would miss him very much and hope they could continue to be good friends by communicating to each other through letters.

Ah Man was devastated. Mei Mei was the woman of his dreams. He had big plans to share with her. Now everything was shattered. He felt something in him had died, a fire extinguished. He felt cold. He was in Nanjing alone, working in a heavily guarded underground bunker. He could not get away soon enough to talk to Mei Mei face-to-face, to make her understand the importance of their work to redeem their motherland and, more importantly, how much he needed her, how much he loved her.

Suddenly everything seemed bleak and hopeless. He felt betrayed by her false promises. *This was the end*, he thought.

In 1928 Ah Man was in Shanghai again, working as a journalist during the day and at night working with the political comrades to plan strategy and gather resources for the future battles.

This year the Nationalist Party (NP) started the process of creating a dictatorship government with the goal of seizing the entire country.

From then on the CCP and NP were locked in constant battles in different cities. Ah Man lived near the headquarters of the NP, and as a result, it was not too difficult for him to obtain information here and there through his old university colleagues and friends and through the international media core, who were also doubling as spies scattered all over China. Meanwhile, he had established a rather wide network, covering different classes of society from the superrich bankers to, and including, the dusty old beggar on the back street corner that no one noticed.

By this time Chan Ah Man could read, write, and speak fluent Mandarin, Japanese, and English. In his tiny one-room flat, in the dark alley street behind the grand lights of the dream city, Ah Man wrote reports on his discoveries. He wrote that the NP had superior arms and airplanes, a well-trained air force, good military organisation, money and support from the rich warlords who wanted to stick to the land under their control, as well as a superpower, America.

The CCP, on the other hand, was poorly-funded by Russia and far behind in their weapons stock. Their weapons were old, outdated, slow, and always insufficient. They did not even have an air force. They were outgunned, outmanned, out bombed and out fired. They lost one battle after another and were being pushed further and further away from central China to remote areas in the west, to Hubei and Hunan.

A Double Career

During this time, Ah Man plunged himself totally into his work. He believed in the cause of liberation of China from foreign power and land reform for farmers. A communal system seemed a good idea.

One united China in peace would be a wonderful dream, and this dream was worth fighting for, even dying for. He offered himself to be a spy for his political party and at the same time still working for his newspaper company.

He could do both and collect two salaries. He needed to save a lot of money, because he owed a lot to his family. His promise to his father and big brother never left his mind. From then on Ah Man would travel back and forth between cities, sometimes using messengers in the underground network to relay up-to-date reports on the movement of the NP camp.

This was a very dangerous time for all the enemies of General Chiang because at this point in time he was at the height of his power. He collected smaller warlords under his wings and ruthlessly crushed those who opposed him. Through this exercise he had gained much land and resources, and province after province promised allegiance to him and his party.

In the cities, Chiang and his police would use violence whenever and wherever it suits them. They would shut down newspapers, shops, bookstores, and any organisation that he suspected to be against him. People were kidnapped and tortured and disappeared on a daily basis. Ah Man worked through a close-knit network of old school friends who had the same ideals and interests, as well as undercover members who infiltrated the local government or the NP itself.

Sometimes he would receive news that one or more of his colleagues had been caught, tortured, and executed. He himself also had a few narrow escapes.

On this fateful day his newspaper company was ransacked and torched. His secret identity had been uncovered. Just when he was about to leave, he heard a bang and immediately we felt a rod of heat and pain in one of his leg. Another shot and he was down, struggling to breathe as the flame and smoke engulfed the office. He fainted.

He could have died there and then if not for a colleague who arrived just in time and dragged Ah Man's limp body away from the fire. When he came to, he saw that he was tended by a doctor in a private clinic. He was told that he was shot twice, once on the shoulder and another in the left leg. Bullets were extracted, but he lost a lot of blood and the inhalation of the poisonous fume would take longer to heal.

Then a friendly face appeared, a comrade in arms. He told Ah Man that he was told about the impeding attack and to go to warn Ah Man and to take him away. Unfortunately, his errand was delayed by road blocks and arrests by the militia. By the time he arrived, he saw Ah Man already on the ground surrounded by tongues of fire.

Moreover, he said that the spy cover was off, but the NP people were not searching for him because they thought he was dead.

In any case, it was not safe for him to stay in China. He will be shipped to British colony Hong Kong, and there he will remain pending for further instruction.

It was a long and arduous journey to Hong Kong, and Ah Man collapsed a few times. Finally, his friend brought him to a small house in an unfamiliar area.

He asked his friend, "Where is this place? I had been to Hong Kong before, but this is new to me."

His friend replied, "This is called the Wall City. This part is known as the No Man's Land. This lies beyond the border of Hong Kong and China. The rule of law is out of bounds here, therefore a refuge for the fugitives, the criminals, the smugglers, the gangsters, and, of course, spies. You will be safe here."

And so under the shaded umbrella of the Wall City, Ah Man slowly recuperated and heal; however, his left leg never fully recovered and for the rest of his life he would be walking with a limp.

After one year, he was ready to leave and was brought to Macau, a Portuguese colony. There he met more of his CCP comrades, and soon he was being transported back to the Mainland quietly.

From this time onward, he would change his name and identity often. Only his boss and no one else in the city knew his real identity or where he would stay at any given time. He would move from city to city and province to province, collecting and relaying information.

He was a man who lived in the shadows. He was a lonely figure, working mostly at night and underground. He was a different person to different people. He was a chameleon. Sometimes, when the pursuit was too hot, he would put on a disguise and make the long icy journey to the Himalaya mountains in the north, while other times he would go to Hong Kong or Macau. One time he even went to Japan posing as a Japanese journalist, as he was fluent in Japanese.

In 1933 another heartbreaking event occurred. Ah Man received a letter from home. His mother had died after months of bedridden illness. Her death had brought deep grief in Ah Man's heart. Miraculously, this pain of loss, instead of propelling him into cold and darkness, boosted his passion to bring goodness to the Chinese people. The light of his compassion grew to new heights. He could not even understand this spiritual transformation, but he felt a renewed strength as the war deepened.

Finally, one day, in October 1933, under constant land and air raids and bombardments, the CCP with its eighty thousand people packed their belongings and started the exodus of three thousand miles into the deepest part of China. This was the Long March. Ah Man was there.

During the next year or so, the march pushed forward despite constant fighting against heavy military roadblocks set up by the NP; and on top of that there was also starvation, exhaustion, and disease that killed most of the people, though many also deserted.

From the eighty thousand that originally started, only four thousand people arrived at their final destination one year later. Ah Man survived, but only just. He was frail, starving, and his leg wound was painful and slowed his progress; but his passion to liberate China from foreign power and total land reform continued in his heart. He would fight on until it became a reality. He would not give up.

In this quiet rural place, far away from the chaotic front, the CCP slowly recuperated. By collaborating with the local farmers and poor people along their journey, they had harvested much support and sympathy, included men willing to fight on the same front.

Through the help of an influential friend, a high-ranking military officer, his family and some of his old neighbours were transferred to a new farm in a safe zone far from war. This time they owned the land. Ah Man was now far away from his family. He was staying with another farm family in a village nearby, recuperating and also waiting for instructions for his next assignment.

In 1937 Ah Man was sent back to the city to dig for more information. China had plunged deeper into darkness, devastation, and bloodshed with no end in sight. Ah Man reported that Japan had launched a full-scale invasion in China. Chiang and some warlords tried to battle the Japanese but to no avail. City after city fell, from Beijing to Shanghai.

From 1938 to 1939 Ah Man followed the Japanese movement. They pushed south, taking Nanjing, Guangzhou, Hong Kong, and thereafter controlled all the important coastal ports and economic centres of China. All this time, Ah Man travelled with the Japanese secretly, going through He was present at every new Japanese conquest. He could infiltrate or intercept many of the Japanese messages, often posing as a Japanese journalist.

Ah Man informed his comrades that after the fall of Shanghai, Chiang planned to escape to Chongqing and would stay there but was secretly dealing both with Moscow and Washington at the same time. Ah Man discovered that he continued to harbour the policy of ruling China alone and would not rest until he had totally wiped out the CCP.

During a short period of time, the Japanese ruled most of China's main economic centres and there was a false sense of ceasefire and calmness.

Meanwhile, Ah Man received instructions to stay in Shanghai and watch the movement of the Japanese. He was also to travel to Chongqing regularly and to report on Chiang's camp.

Japan Surrender and the Real Battle Begins

In 1945 great news arrived by way of a secret telegram that Ah Man's group intercepted.

It read: "Japan surrendered to the American ending the Second World War, but not before the H-bomb was dropped on their home soil. They released China to the higher power, America."

Ah Man rushed this great news to his comrades who began to come out from their hiding places to grab the stockpile of military hardware that had been left behind by the Japanese.

This time, the battle line was clear and drawn. Russia was backing the CCP, while America was backing the NP. The battle for one united China had begun. The looming black cloud that hung over China grew ever darker and bigger, harbouring a thunder within that was ready to release its wrath to the land and its people below.

In 1947 a full-blown civil war exploded in China. The People's Liberation Army under the CCP marched south of Harbin. Meanwhile, the Nationalist camp under Chiang, which was stationed in Shanghai and other cities, drew its resources from industries, banks, and the superrich who migrated mostly to America but continued to support the NP so that their properties would be secured when they return.

There was widespread corruption, decadence, and waste. In Shanghai, under Chiang, inflation was 500 percent and there was famine, unrest, protest, imprisonment and killings. There were also constant strikes by workers, who were switching to the CCP camp in great numbers, all which contributed to the collapse of Chiang's regime.

The CCP camp covered all the rural territories, collecting farmers, their agriculture resources, and the labourers, and generally all those who were unhappy, which was plenty. By accumulating piles of modern weapons, especially airplanes, looted from the Japanese, plus new recruits of pilots, the balance between the two sides gradually became more even. There was one more piece of good news from Ah Man: the Americans were closing their money tap on Chiang. Their rampant corruption, poor financial management, and unstoppable greed disgusted even the friendliest of American officials. Besides, a new president had been elected and this one did not find Chiang a worthy ally and the new policy was to shut off the money supply.

This new policy broke the camel's back, and from then on the Nationalists found themselves losing battles and territory one after another to the People's Liberation Army (PLA) until finally they were driven out of the mainland totally and ended up on the small island of Taiwan. Despite many attempts and appeals for America to help him recuperate his loss so that he could crush the enemy and grab the throne in Bei Jing, Chiang never set foot on the mainland again. He died in Taiwan.

After the war Ah Man retreated to his one-room apartment in the backstreet of Shanghai central and read the newspaper about the celebration. His direct line of communication with his comrade was cut and so was his monthly salary. He was not bitter about this; instead, he was grateful, because most ex-spies he knew had got a bullet in the head as a final reward. No one likes a living spy who could still talk when the job was over. He was spared.

Ah Man's days of spying, of hiding, and living with constant fear was over. He could finally throw away his battered travelling shoes and put down his pen. All through his life he witnessed a weak and fragmented China and he was hopeful that from now on his country would be whole again. He hoped that the Chinese people, who had suffered so much throughout the volatile decades, would enjoy peace and prosperity.

Silently deep within himself Ah Man said a prayer and asked for forgiveness from all those men and women that he had killed. Even though he did not pull the trigger he killed through the information about the enemies. Indirectly, he had killed many and his heart felt heavy. He made a promise that this was the end of this abhorrent behaviour. Indeed, war is not only destructive to material matter, it is much more detrimental to the souls.

After the land reform law was passed, there were no more private owners. Instead, all land belonged to the government and farmers could lease land from it. It was time to pay another visit to his family again.

He had helped his father get a bigger plot of land with a ninety-nine- year lease and more animals, plus a small fishpond. Then he withdrew, from a special hiding place, all the money he had earned and saved during the last twenty-five years to build a brand-new house for his father, plus an extra wing for his brother and his family. He paid back the money he owed to big brother, Ah Long, and set up an education fund so that his nieces and nephews could go to school in the future. He had kept his promise.

After everything was settled, Ah Man sat down to his last meal with his family.

"Would you stay with the family for good this time?" his brother had asked.

Ah Man had thought long and hard about this question before he came home.

"No," he answered finally. "I've been living in the city for too long. Rural life is too quiet and the air too fresh and clean for me now." Everybody laughed and said it was so silly.

His father, who was eighty-seven years old and was still actively participating in farmwork, looked lean, suntanned, and mentally alert. His clean lifestyle; fresh air; sunshine; and good, natural food could easily stretch his age to a hundred.

He could easily outlive me, Ah Man thought.

After years of living dangerously, Ah Man had aged prematurely. He was hunched, pale, his ever-present limp, and he coughed, often aching all over.

The next day he spent some time talking with his father and then said goodbye to everyone and started the long journey back to the city. His work here was done, and he felt relieved.

Back in his little flat, he felt a strange heavy fatigue, which seemed to descend upon his body, sinking very low and very deep. He had never felt so tired before, and now all he wanted was to rest.

He thought, *I need to sleep very deeply for a long time.* He was fifty-seven years old.

Next morning, his neighbour brought Ah Man's usual breakfast, consisting of soy milk and fried dough and found him still in bed, which was unusual. It seemed that he was in a deep relaxed sleep. When his friend went closer to touch him, he realised that Ah Man had died. His face was smooth and peaceful. He had passed away quietly the night before during his sleep.

THE ASTRAL WORLD

The First Station

During that night's sleep, Ah Man dreamt that he rose from his body. He was separated from his body and then he looked at it as it lay on the bed.

"Is this a dream, or is he truly leaving?" he asked himself.

He turned away from the body and saw a small tunnel. There was a light at the end of it. Suddenly he felt he was being pulled, ever so gently, into this tunnel; and soon he was in a sphere of white light. The light was not from a sun or any shinning source; rather, it was more like a sphere with a total absence of darkness. He heard the sound of faint soothing music in the atmosphere. He stood there for a while, a bit lost.

What is this *place?* he *th*ought. What is happening? Is this a dream?

Soon he saw someone approaching. Gradually, he recognised him. He was his beloved teacher and guide, Purple Flame. Suddenly he realised who he truly was. He was Sprkle. Ah Man was the body on the bed. He had left the physical body and his temporal identity.

Purple Flame was now standing next to him. He extended his Light Body and embraced Sprkle as a sign of welcome with love. In this embrace, he felt a warm connection and a very good sensation. Sprkle found his natural ability to communicate telepathically.

"What is this place?" he asked his teacher.

His teacher explained, "This is the lower astral world, a transit station for all recently arrived souls. Here you will rest because, after decades of living on Earth, there are memories and information that need to be analysed and dealt with. The soul body needs to be cleansed. There are emotional issues that need to be settled in the conscious mind and released. Heavy matters stuck to the soul memory need to be transformed. This is the cleansing period. Depending on the attachment of the soul to earthly materials, this period can go from one to thousands of Earth years.

"Some souls are so attached to their Earth life relation or unsettled issues that they would opt to stay in this lower astral world briefly and request for reincarnation again as soon as possible. Others would also stay briefly, but after releasing emotional "baggage," would move on to a higher plane of the astral world. Here, there would be more light, the energy would be less heavy, and the vibration would be higher. There would be a deeper cleansing and reflection in preparation for a return to the spirit world. As long as the soul is still in the astral plane, then he is still in his soul body, which is the vehicle for this sphere, just as the physical body is required to function in a three-dimensional sphere like Earth.

"When the soul is ready and willing to return to his spirit home in the fifth dimension, he will go through a further process and he will discard his soul body to reveal his true body of Pure Light. At this point he will take only the extracted memories, which will be stored in crystal light particles. All these memories will require the help and much work of the Transformation Specialist, whom you will meet when it is required."

Sprkle asked, "Teacher, how come this time I was not able to turn my body to a point of light and return to home base like before?"

The teacher said, "This time is different because this journey was a hard one and also we want you to experience the process of after death for a full physical human. This is another lesson for you.

"I will accompany and lead you every step of the way, with one crucial condition: you would have to be willing to go back home. If you chose to stay as a soul and continue in the astral plane, at whatever level, then I would respect your wish and make it possible. And if your choice is to reincarnate, then that would also be arranged. This time, the whole process would be much quicker than the first time, because you are already in soul body.

"First things first, do you need time to rest? If you do, I can bring you to a quiet resting place. You call me when you are ready to talk about your experience."

The Cleansing Session

Sprkle did not feel tired. After leaving the heavy physical body, he felt his body to be lighter and able to float anywhere he wished. A new energy had filled his body.

He told his teacher that he would like a cleansing session and may need a brief time to be by himself, his soul self. Almost instantly, he found himself standing at the entrance of a chamber with colourful crystals.

In front of him stood a giant transparent crystal, so big that he could not even see the edge of this mysterious stone. As he stood in front of it, Sprkle could see a light inside the stone. First, it was white colour and looked small and feeble, then it began to move round and round inside the stone, dancing elegantly. Gradually, it changed into a multitude of colours. The colours were strange, the like of which Sprkle had never seen before. This light continued to move. It swirled and danced, with one colour playing a dominant role and then would fade and another colour would dominate, but all the time they would be mixing and dancing with each other. Sprkle could not tell how many colours there were. He just stood there mesmerised. This light then gently reached out from the stone to dance around him, moving from top to bottom and covering him completely. It then formed a smooth, soothing, multicoloured cocoon with Sprkle inside, like a foetus in a womb. It was so comforting, so warm, and so much love filled his heart that he felt as though his heart chakra was bursting forward with a million love flowers.

Sprkle could not remember when he last felt so good, so calm, so secured, so protected, and so peaceful.

Everything is being taken care of, he thought. The Mighty Presence and the Cosmic Spiritual Masters are keeping balance of all life. He totally surrendered his last drop of attachment and worries, and he slipped into a deep slumber in this wonderful cocoon.

Life Lessons Review

Time cycles turned. When he awoke, he found himself standing next to his teacher again. They were in a small amphitheatre. The sky in front was the stage and screen, and at the moment it was blank. They were ready to go through the full memory bank of his immediate lifetime and discuss the lessons learned.

As soon as Sprkle could focus, he began to see images on the night sky. He could see a pregnant woman, the womb inside her, cells were dividing, a foetus was forming, then a baby boy. Then, like in a movie, he saw the baby Chan Ah Man being born, his first step, his first word, and so forth. Bit by little bit he remembered this life journey. He was watching the images, yet at the same time he was also experiencing every moment, every thought, and every feeling that was being played out before him.

He and Chan Ah Man seemed to be one. Yet, as Sprkle watched everything, his perception was much wider and deeper. He remembered everything—the expectations and disappointments, the joy and heartbreaks in his relationships with Mei Mei and his mother, the two women closest to him. He felt again the adrenaline rush when he was being chased by secret police and how he fled many times to escape the Nationalist noose that was constantly hanging just above his head. He relived his fear, his courage, his ideals, his crushing remorse with the realization of causing deaths for hundreds of people whom he thought to be his enemies and also friends whom he had lied to and betrayed. Every thought, every word, every intention was revealed.

Purple Flame sat by his side, patiently watching the changing images. Sometimes Sprkle would freeze a frame and ask his teacher to explain the purpose and meaning of that particular situation. Together they went through all the minute details of everything that had happened during this short life journey. They covered intentions, thoughts, actions, consequences, reactions, guilt, and forgiveness. They also analysed emotional issues that had not been addressed and settled.

Purple Flame then explained about the life lessons that Sprkle might like to muse upon.

Courage

"Courage was summoned when you took your first step out of the family's home village into the unknown when you went to the city school. Thereafter, more courage was needed when you went to Shanghai, where you felt like a frog out of a well, and then when you went to join the Communist party when the Nationalist was at its height of power. Again, courage was constantly summoned during your long and dangerous career as a spy in a period when China was at its most violent, most bloody, most inhuman, and most cruel. War and battles were almost a daily affair. To be willing to face your challenges and to be able to look fear in the face and overcome it is courage. This is the building block for a strong soul and spirit."

Loyalty and Perseverance

"During a period when a country is being invaded by a foreign power and its own government is powerless, corrupt, and fragmented, people would ask, 'To which direction do I go? Do I follow the most powerful, even though they are selfish and cruel, just to stay safe? Or do I choose one party that leads to self-sacrifice for the betterment of the people and reunification of my country?'

"It is not easy to choose wisely when the adversary is powerful. You chose well, and you stayed true to your belief, despite the fact that the consequence of your choice of spying for the CCP put your life in constant danger. The situation was that of poverty, war, misery, and constantly changing and confusing scenarios in the political arena. Life conditions like these create fear, hatred, doubts, mistrust, lies, and other negative vibrations so strong that it would be easy to throw anyone off course. You never changed your party. You stayed on your path, up until the very end of your life. You held on tightly to your belief.

"This is loyalty, and this is perseverance. You passed this test by showing your full commitment to the cause and to accomplish your mission, despite the hardship."

Relationships on the Physical Level

"From the first breath you took as a human, you were separated from the spiritual world and you plunged into the darkness of amnesia. Like a blind man, you needed to feel your way and work on your return to connect with love/light and your own soul and spirit. This is quite a challenge for all souls.

"With your mother, it was unconditional love with emotional attachment, experienced deeply as a child. Then you went out into the world and lost that feeling. It became forgotten. Then you visit your mother for the last time, and the time of parting had an intense emotional transfer for both of you. Your mother had managed to touch your heart so deeply that you remembered the meaning of true love, the universal love, which is the essence of your own soul/spirit. That was why you cried so deeply. It was this love that brought you back to us.

"Other points on relationships are also important. Your relationship with Mei Mei, even though brief, played a significant role during the most crucial of time. Here, on the other hand, was a kind of romantic, idealist illusion that you had, mistaking it to be love. You wanted Mei Mei, to possess her, to have her fight alongside with you, to help you, to make you happy. That was wrong. Mei Mei could never make you happy. Only *you* can find happiness within yourself. You cannot possess another person for that would be slavery.

"When Mei Mei left you, the feeling of loss, even anger and betrayal, rose in you. Why? Because you felt that she did not deliver what you expected of her. You dreamed of marrying her, of setting up a family home with her, as this meant happiness for you. Well, all that crashed in your mind.

"You see now the meaning of true love and false love? Your relationship with the party members, working in shadows, all your hard work, had not been acknowledged, rewarded or appreciated. You died an unknown hero. Are you bitter about this? Do you feel this is an issue that needs to be settled?

"How about the enemies in the NP camp, the Japanese and other foreign devils that you so hated and wanted to destroy? How many of these people died indirectly through you? What lessons do you think these relationships bring to your table? What wisdom can you extract from this experience?"

Altruism

"You chose well, Sprkle," said his teacher at the end of the session, "both for the time and the place. For the political setting in China had never changed so quickly, had never been so chaotic. You also chose your profession well, being a spy at this point in time would play a crucial part in changing the political and military condition in China. Your work was dangerous. Your hard-earned contribution was not publicly recognised or rewarded, but deep in the heart of the people, they will know one day that, through your work, and many like you, the unification of China was made possible, that peace was achievable at the end.

"You provided your family with a better quality of life, and more importantly, you set up a foundation for proper education for the children of your brother, even though you did not have any of your own. This is self-sacrifice. This is altruism."

Forgiveness

"Now this is the most important lesson of all. Sprkle, you had chosen to be in physical human body during a very challenging time. Therefore, you focused mostly on your own needs and your own survival. Especially during the period of your work as a spy. You had shut down your emotions and even your higher spiritual mental body. All you saw was what you needed to do to accomplish your mission. You were not aware of the people that you had hurt, whether directly or indirectly. You had betrayed and lied to many people, and yet you were not aware that you were also being betrayed by your friends and colleagues. You had chosen to descend to the dark world of war and suffering to be one of the dark force itself.

"This was the game you chose to play, and you must know that for every action there is consequence, and this would boomerang back to you sooner or later. This is the unspoken rule of the game. This journey is over now, and you must remember to forgive yourself, forgive those whom you had hurt, and forgive those who had hurt you. Only through forgiveness that your mind and soul is set free. Remember, this all-important lesson. Well, my dear one, you wanted action and you got it, yes?"

Sprkle smiled and said, "Never a dull moment!"

When this exercise was finished, Purple Flame took Sprkle to another sphere. His teacher said that he could meet anyone he wished in this immediate past life, those who had died and already returned and also those who are still living on Earth. He reminded Sprkle that souls only take part of its Light Body for incarnation. All those in his group are still living in the transit zone, pending their decision to return to 3D Earth or not.

Soul Group Reunion

Sprkle said that he wanted to meet his people, and soon he was in a big hall full of people. A party was going on, with familiar music. Some people were dancing, others talking. It was a merry and joyful atmosphere, a celebration.

He walked into the room, and those near the entrance saw him. He recognised them and greeted them and soon everybody in the hall stood very still and looked at him and smiled. As he moved further into the hall, one by one he saw their familiar faces. They were all in China with him. This was a celebration especially for Sprkle. This was a welcome home party just for him.

There was the soul that played the role of his mother. There was his father, who was still on Earth, and also the one who played the role of Mei Mei and a host of all those friends; schoolmates; colleagues in the newspaper firm; his comrades-in-arms; his friends who had died of starvation, who were captured, those who were tortured, killed, blown to pieces during gun battles; and also those who were his enemies, the Nationalists, the Japanese, the Americans, etc. Literally everyone who had crossed his path was there.

He went up to the soul who was his mother. They greeted each other with a special smile. Her body was now an egg shape of beautiful light of yellow, gold, and light blue. Her soul name was Solya, and she had a strong female energy. She was old and wise, and her aura had a deep blue halo, which signified deep wisdom gained through many reincarnations and experiences. She came from a faraway sphere deep in space, a place out of reach for Sprkle at this point. He thanked her for her love, so deep and powerful, that guided him back to his spirit. It was this unconditional love for this mother that had dominated Chan Ah Man's last thought before he died.

She was happy to be of service. Chan Ah Man was easy to love. He was pure and innocent and full of curiosity about everything, yet he was strong and determined. Solya loved the experience and would be happy to join him on another adventure when needed. She will soon return to her deep-space world.

Next, he came face-to-face with Mei Mei. They looked at each other and laughed. They now understood that their separation had to be. Chan A Man could not be married and raise a family. I t was not written that way. Their friendship served an important foundation for Chan Ah Man to dive into the political arena with passion and courage, especially when they decided together to register at the party in Shanghai, making it official their political intention. It was much easier with her fanning his fire at the time, because the night before this happened, he had nightmares and was full of fears and doubts.

Mei Mei, whose soul name was Airon, also had a dominant female energy structure. Her aura was slightly yellow and pink. She was in fact not from his group. She came in from another sphere on a visit to play out this life episode with Sprkle. A temporary assistant, so to speak.

After this party, she would return to her group, which consisted of slightly more mature souls then Sprkle's group. She congratulated him on a successful mission and she said that if he continues to learn with such fervour and commitment he would soon be promoted to a higher sphere to join a more mature soul group.

Standing next to her was another familiar energy. She was his sister, Ah Jan. She had almost the same aura colour like Airon, and she came from the same sphere and same group. Her soul name was Aireen. She reminded Sprkle of his first female encounter, Nan. Aireen had this gentle, kind, and infinitely patient characteristic about her aura. He thanked her for her tender loving care when he was small, a crucial foundation for building self-confidence and courage for his future career. Indeed, she was his second mother, and without her support, he may not have made it. Aireen was modest in saying that it was simply her agreement and she was just fulfilling that. She added that, as a matter of fact, she loved her experience in taking care of the young ones and she was now considering making this her soul career, like Nan, only that she would like to do it on Earth. So many children needed love and tender nourishment on this planet, and she had so much love that she could give, and give inexhaustibly.

Sprkle admired this noble thought and wished her well and great success.

As Aireen and Airon moved away, Sprkle saw a familiar soul, predominantly male energy, with a very strong and powerful magnetic field. This aura was colourful yet deep and indescribable. He was drawn to it like a nail to a magnet, and instantly stood face-to-face with the person he knew as his boss. At that point in time, his physical body was still living on Earth, wreaking another wave of havoc with the cultural evolution in China. As a soul in astral world, however, he was just one of a myriad of souls. He also came from another sphere, different from Solya. He was sort of on loan to play out the China episode with Sprkle.

His telepathic exchange was fast and strong. He made it known to Sprkle that he did not have a name, meaning that nothing can be written in language form. He actually belonged to a sphere bordering the edge of the Milky Way galaxy. Sprkle felt that his energy was very powerful with the potential to be very extreme, either negative or positive, and also there were elements in his light crystal body that were totally foreign and unreadable to him. Nevertheless, he found him very interesting and felt deep respect.

He also congratulated Sprkle for a well-played game. It was very intense, yet very meaningful. He asked if Sprkle understood why he had not been contacted or given any recognition for his contribution to the success of the CCP. He replied that he was not bitter. He accepted this fact and was even grateful for not having been given a bullet in the head like the rest of his spies.

"Well, they needed to be silenced for security, that was a professional hazard, so to speak," and the boss chuckled slyly.

Sprkle smiled mildly but did not really understand what he meant. He then turned around and saw his father. His soul name was Airoon. He came from the same sphere as Airon. He thanked Sprkle for the opportunity to participate in this game plan because he needed to reincarnate on Earth for his further learning. His lessons were appreciation and human relationship. He had never incarnated with a family before. He was often a monk or a nun, or a hermit, and had experienced many lifetimes of lone journeys. This past life had been very challenging for him. It was very hard to raise and sustain a family in turbulent and famine- stricken China. He was still there, plodding daily, although it was much better now, and life was easier. He said that he would be coming back soon, as he only had a couple of Earth years to go. Soon he floated off to join Airon and Aireen.

Sprkle looked around him and saw all those great and wise souls with colourful auras and those like him, young and innocent, with a pure white aura. There was no enemy or boss or torturer, only brothers and sisters— children of one Great Central Light, the ever-existing Presence. They were all there to greet him, to welcome him home, even though this was only a temporary home.

He moved in to embrace his own group souls. Joy and gratitude filled his heart. They all laughed, and the music began to play, and they started dancing or prancing about, shooting colourful lights like laser guns all over the sky. Then they all talked about their experiences and laughed at the big game plan, the reincarnation hall, and the Specialist.

Some souls even started to talk about going back to Earth to do reverse role play. Those who were rich now wanted to be poor. Those who were beaten by others now wanted to be the aggressor. Those who were men now wanted to be female. The talk went on and on. The party was in a joyful, playful mood.

After the party Spkle returned to the Hall of Records to find out more about the current event of the planet.

END TIME

As soon as Sprkle arrived at the Hall of Universal Record, he resumed his observation of the political crisis on Earth.

From the last image before he left, he saw that the scientists were on the verge of discovering the making of the nuclear bomb. That was in America. On the global eastern front, he saw Japan had already invaded one part of China, even though an official full scale invasion had not yet taken place. All the signs were on the wall that this would be the next step. On the European front, Germany was totally prepared to go on a full- scale military campaign to the East and to the West. They wanted all of Europe, Russia, even Africa, literally from sea to shiny sea.

Behind the public news media and the propaganda, the Elite Group was watching, funding all the power players, be it Japan, China, Germany, Russia, the Middle Eastern kingdoms, and so forth. All those who were willing to kill, to bomb, to create chaos were welcome and given total support in terms of finance and weapons.

All was prepared, and the plan was for America to come in last, save the day, and be the hero of the world at the same time control all the nations from then on.

The world would be under their feet. The world populace is their willing slaves, to be manipulated in any way they see fit. From then on there will be one nation, one world order, under the Elite Group; and they were rubbing their hands with glee and anticipation.

However, Sprkle saw on the holographic image right behind and above the Elite Group there was another group of beings, not human beings, but ETs, a conglomeration of ETs from different star systems and even from higher dimensions. This group is of a bigger, darker, more menacing, more evil, the ever-present POWR Federation, the true power behind the thrones. They are the real lords of the world because they were infiltrating and controlling the minds of the Elite Group. They were dictating the whole war plan to the Elite members and their generals. They were the ones who are feeding them the latest technologies for better military hardware and the ideas to build all kinds of weapons that cause mass destruction.

To the eyes of Sprkle, who had seen so many wars throughout the long history of this planet from ancient to modern time, this so-called World War II is just another one created by the Dark Force, the Fallen Angels who had since the beginning of time positioned themselves on the opposite side of the chessboard.

The negative force against the positive force.

Suddenly, through the holographic image, he saw an explosion somewhere in Europe, and all hell broke loose. And soon fire was everywhere, and mass horrible butchery committed, countries devouring each other. Earth was burning again, and needless to say hundreds of millions of people perished.

Then the mother of all bombs were dropped in Japan, one in Hiroshima and another in Nagasaki. It was instant and total decimation for all life in the immediate cities. The intense heat and fire spread immediately, turning everything to dust like a horrible harvest of death. What remained was further wiped out by the following radiation poison in the air. Through water and wind pollution, the populace of the whole Japanese country suffered deeply for a long time and for many generations.

The American got their ultimate test, their answer for the extent of destruction this kind of bombs can reach. Those who possess this kind of power is the master of the world. In the most morbid of ways, this experiment had wet their appetite for more.

From then on it was a global military weapon race to get the nuclear bomb and later the hydrogen bomb. The Soviet Union was the second to reach the top, and from then on it was the question of who has more nuclear war heads, nuclear submarines, nuclear rockets, and so forth.

Following the US and the Soviet Union, other smaller countries and nations were clamoring for a piece of the pie.

From a distance, Sprkle could see the madness in the minds of the human beings who could not see for themselves that they were racing toward their very own suicide, a worldwide . . .

Nuclear Armageddon

And then the Angelic Council stepped in. This is not the time for young human beings to play with dangerous "toys." This is Ascension time, and no one is allowed to interfere with it.

Next Sprkle noticed that throughout the 1950s and 1960s many military bases and laboratories around the world that were involved with either nuclear or hydrogen bombs were being dismantled and shut down as if by magic. The workers would often see extraterrestrial ships in the sky hovering above those facilities before the breakdown of the systems occurred.

Seeing this, Sprkle breathed a sigh of relief. He thought, *Oh my God, that was close. What were these human beings thinking?*

Purple Flame came, and he said, "This world war is not just on this level. This war is being fought on all dimensions as far up to the eighth dimension, and also many parts of the Milky Way galaxy is also involved, and even some systems in the Andromeda Galaxy are not spared.

"This is the war of all the wars since ancient times. This is the last chance to capture the star gates before the Ascension time set in and after that the gates will be closed. When that happens those who could rise will do that, and those who could not make it will be doomed to fall to a lower spiral or trapped in a parallel planet in the same dimension. So the Dark Force will try their very best to secure all their domain and more before the gates close.

"My dear Sprkle, I can see that your focus has always been on the planet Earth, but you must extend your vision to the fact that the Ascension time line is a cosmic event. In order to see a bigger picture of the situation, you have to extend the time line that you are following to a higher and wider scope. Meaning you have to not only follow the 3D Line, but also the 4D and 5D Line. Like so."

Having said that, Purple Flame drew some symbols and uttered some sounds and the holographic Universal Record started to open in layers. They looked like worlds within worlds, and they were alive, growing, and changing constantly.

The sheer immensity of what was in front and around Sprkle made him feel totally lost and entranced. He was just awestruck, his mind swirling in pure wonderment.

Next, he saw Purple Flame reached out his arm into one of the holographic world, muttered a few words, drew a few symbols, and a few lines appeared in front of him. Sprkle saw that these holographic lines had living things and light in them. They were the life lines and time lines that were "woven" into the "tapestry" of the Hall of Universal Remembrance. Then carefully Purple Flame guided Sprkle's hand along those chosen lines and drew a few symbols on them and immediately they turned into a disc.

Purple Flame said, "Now we can go back to your home base and watch these lessons."

In an instant they were back on Sprkle's familiar sphere. Purple Flame took out the disk, drew a symbol with his finger on it, and immediately the holograph images sprang to life.

The teacher then said, "Now, my dear, you must understand by now those war and peace, destruction and construction, the death and rebirth are just mere cycles of the so-called Wheel of Fortune, the Wheel of Life Changes. It so happens that on this solar system the level of disasters and violence had been turned up a few notches in comparison to other systems. Well, the big picture is the nature of Creation itself. The Source of Life, means all kinds of life. I am opening an image of the universe for you to see. What can you see?"

"I can see movements and colours. A very big spectrum of colours." "Yes, behind the colours there is what? There is darkness, which is a part of the picture. Darkness and Light, like electrical and magnetic energy. The interplay of these two aspects is the basis of creation.

"As there are many layers of light frequencies, there are many layers of darkness as well. And from here you can see the potential for variations—infinite variety of manifestation of cosmic energy. As simple as mixing the colour of yellow and blue produce green. If you expand your mind from this concept, then you may have a glimpse of what creation and co- creation means.

"So from this higher perspective, there is no opposition of good and bad or the Dark Force versus the Guardians. Everything is and will ever be within the Sphere of the One Source of Life. Do you understand that, Sprkle?

"Both the Dark Force and the Masters of Light on the highest level of the spiritual realm are watching as the progression unfolds. They would not interfere with the evil ways of the Dark Force unless they overstep the limit of allowance set up by the Creation of the Universe. Even they know the rules. Do you have any question, my dear?"

"You know me, I have always tons of questions, but for now I am just worried about Earth meeting the time line."

"Well, if you move the time line forward to around the year 2000, the new Earth millennia, you will see that much of the planet has been rebuilt with new modern architecture. The human population has increased exponentially to over six billion. Also new technology has been introduced after the war especially after 1960s, and if you look at the communication devices since the 1990s, you will be surprised to see how fast and wide information has been able to reach the populace. They call it the Internet. "Apart from that, other technology had been discovered and applied such as time travel, antigravity technology, free energy devices, remote viewing ability, the planetary portals had been frequently used to travel to other planets and solar systems. Mars and many moons and satellites beyond the solar systems have been occupied and shared space with other ETs for space trading and even space industries. Unfortunately, these are mostly used by the military elite group and big businesses. The mass population of the world was totally blocked from this knowledge. But in the near future, this secret wall will crumble and truth will prevail."

Sprkle was happy to see the extent of information being shared. He saw that even though the Dark Side also use these facilities to spread their evil ways, but this system is being used generally in a positive way, especially to expose government secrets and mind control systems, which was kept from the populace before. Exposure and revelation is one of the best thing that is happening to the world these days. Human beings are sharing, communicating like never before.

"What about the time line? Will Earth be on board or not?" Spkle asked earnestly.

The teacher calmly replied, "Move time forward to 2012–2017, my dear, and you will see that the danger is over. Yes, finally after waiting for millions of years and thousands of wars, Earth is on the right path.

"Remember the Mayan Lei Line? Well, along these lines many secret and hidden dimensional portals and power base were laid to be used at the right time. These plus the help of benevolent beings from the Aquaferion star systems and their technology of Light, the planetary grid set up by the Dark Force was being burst open and destroyed.

"Mind you, this is no easy task. Battles had been fought very hard indeed by the highest level of Light Warriors against unimaginable destructive power by the Dark Side. The most difficult issue was to avoid total annihilation of the planet on one side and fight the fire power on the other hand. The Dark Side wanted to blow up the whole planet if they could not get it. It was a narrow balance of defensive and offensive at the same time. I think only the best Warriors of Light can achieve that.

"Sprkle, you can say that the danger of falling behind the Ascension Program is over, but you must not celebrate yet, as it is still transition period. Earth needs a lot of healing and cleansing of the miasma, the dark karmic energy left by human—the air, water, land, and food pollution. Much healing work still needs to be done, and this depend of the earthlings. They have to assume the responsibility and clean up the mess they left behind. "The Dark Force is defeated, but its remaining Energy is still lingering around and would still try their best to do harm by inciting a World War III to end it all. With the help of the Galactic Guardian, I think this may not happen but we must still be on guard.

"The Celestial Council of Wisdom has given the Fallen Ones a grace period to return to the fold of Light. After all they are and will always be a part of the First Creation, the Source of Love and Life.

"In any case by 2017, the planet Earth had securely entered the first step into another dimension. It is now in the fourth dimension. This is still transition time, but those earthlings who are ready and willing to go with it would experience a shift in consciousness. Those who opt to stay in the third dimension reality will stay until they are ready to move on in the future."

"What about the twelve lost fragments of Tara? Will there be a closure?" "Ah, you still remember that."

"How can I forget? I was stuck on one of them in space once."

"Ah yes. Well, the eleven planets—Earth (Terra), Mars, Venus, Jupiter, Saturn, Neptune, Mercury, Pluto, Uranus, Nibiru, even the broken Maldack, including Sol itself, will shed off their physical planetary bodies and enter the fourth dimension with their Etheric bodies. And later on, when their vibration is high enough to pass through the dimensional portal to the fifth dimension, they will transform into their astral planetary bodies. From this point on, like pieces of jigsaw puzzles, one by one they will fall into their respective places and affect a full integration with Tara. They have arrived home finally.

"Tara is whole again. Her planetary body exudes tremendous light reaching far and wide into space. She is once again her former brilliant and glorious self. By then she is ready to commence her ascension program to integrate with her sister Gaia on the seventh dimension. It took billions of Earth years to reach this state, but then who is counting, right? In the cosmos all this time is but a wink of an eye. Ha-ha. What do you think, Sprkle?"

"Now I can truly say mission accomplished. Thanks to the tender loving care, the deep unrelenting dedication of all the angels and guardians to make this possible."

"I can see that you have learnt much by observing and following the time lines on the holographic record. Remember this, there are multiverses, multiple time lines with infinite probabilities and parallel realities, thus the nature of the Universal Remembrance, the Tapestry of Life.

"Be patient and go step by step at a time, and you will learn and reach your set goal. I am always with you in spirit."

"Thank you, my dearest teacher, I love you." "Love you too, now go and enjoy your free time."

Sprkle then went alone to sit on his favorite mountain top to watch the stars.

A short time passed, and Purple Flame appeared smiling widely and said to him, "Come, you have been summoned, follow me."

The Violet Chamber and the Gift

Sprkle and Purple Flame came to a big chamber with walls draped with violet light. In the middle of the hall there was a white marble fountain in the shape of a big chalice. It contained crystal-clear magical water. Inside this hall, he could feel a powerful Presence. He could not see the source, but the feeling was very strong.

Behind the fountain sat a group of five Elders. They all wore translucent white robes, and each had an aura of golden white colour. Their faces were clear and yet not clear—it was hard to describe. Sprkle went past the fountain and stood in front of them while his teacher stood behind him to his left, about ten steps away.

"Our dear son, Sprkle," spoke one Elder telepathically. "We welcome you. Your various reincarnations to planet Earth were successful and fruitful. Now let us see what you have been through.

"Ah, you had been an Astral Human on Tara,
as Soul Human at Tangia and also some sea creatures there;
an Urtite student and priest of Ur;
a banana tree briefly;
a female as wife, mother, and grandmother at Mua;
a teacher in Egypt;
and your last journey as a man and spy in China.

"You have done well, and we are all proud of you. Your experiences are our experiences. Your wisdom gained is also our gain, because as you know one is all and all is one. We are of one Mind."

"I thank you for your kindness," replied Sprkle. "I am deeply grateful for the great opportunities given to me. These past incarnations were indeed precious. I have learned much and also ready and willing to learn more. I am not ready to discard this soul body yet. I am willing to reincarnate again, but have not yet decided on the place and form."

The Elder replied, "Before you go, we would like to present you with a gift. Please go to the marble fountain behind you and drink the water there until you feel satisfied."

This Sprkle did, and soon after he had his fill of the magical water. He saw his own light structure changed. It was no longer pure white.

Instead, there was a tinge of yellow and orange, ever so light, but it was there. He was indeed surprised and looked to his teacher, Purple Flame, for explanation; but one of the Elders read his mind and answered him.

"This is the gift. This is your initiation to another level of maturity, meaning you are no longer a baby."

Laughter all around.

"This also means that you will be promoted to a new sphere joining other group with the same vibration. Love and peace be with you."

Purple Flame looked proud and smiled. With a wink of an eye Sprkle was back in his home sphere.

Soon our newly transformed Sprkle found himself sitting alone on top of a pure-blue crystal mountain, suspended in the sky listening to the Music of the Sphere.

From this vantage point, he could see brilliant nebulae, stars, and planets all moving around each other, like jewels dancing in space. Some of them seemed far away while others seemed close enough to touch. They all seemed to be calling to him. From here he would sit and ponder on his next adventure.

End

LAST WORDS

Sitting in my study, looking out to the calm water of the China Pearl River, I realized how wonderful the planet Earth, Terra, is.

The fact that Earth is an open playing field with total freedom of choice for everyone living in or on the ground, be they Reptilians, Greys, Northdics, Insectoids, Humanoids, Hybrids of all kinds, angelic human, angelic beings of other forms, and so forth. All are allowed to follow their own agenda without interference.

Mother Earth/Terra allows itself to be taken down to the darkest pit of destruction and horror and at the eleventh hour managed to stand up and climb back to the Divine Light.

This is a hard school for any soul, no doubt about it, but the result is the kind of diversity in experience that few other planets in the solar system can produce.

This leads me to give honor to the Dark Side, the Fallen Angels, who in the very beginning of time agreed to play the opposite role. Without their evil ways, goodness and love cannot manifest its full potential.

It is in the darkest moments when the light can shine the brightest.

I have incarnated and reincarnated many, many times to experience life on this special planet, and like Sprkle, I have always find it just *marvelous*.

www.ingramcontent.com/pod-product-compliance
Lightning Source LLC
Chambersburg PA
CBHW040828010826
48978CB00012BB/654